OCEAN EARTH

OCEAN EARTH

UNTIL NEXT TIME

Book I of the Ocean Earth Saga

By Sam Terra

Published by Barttek LLC
ISBN: 979-8-9943478-2-9
Copy Editor & Proofreader: Robin Fuller
First Edition: 2025

Dedication

To my wife, my kids, my mom, and my brothers and sister—my built-in support team and comedy panel. I know you'll tell me this book is excellent no matter what anyone else says—and if it isn't, you'll make fun of me just enough to keep me humble and laughing.

This story began as an experiment—part homemade science, part art, and part stubborn faith that even non-professional writers can create something worth reading in this new and wonderful world of AI.

So, dear reader, thank you for giving it a chance. Let's see where this ocean takes us.

Disclaimer

All scientific discussions, theories, and interpretations presented in *Ocean Earth*—including those relating to physics, cosmology, or consciousness—are original imaginative constructs created by the author. They are not derived from, nor affiliated with, any existing scientific institution, publication, or theory beyond general inspiration. These ideas are the intellectual property of the author and are intended solely as elements of creative fiction and philosophical exploration within this narrative.

Preamble

Human creativity has consistently grown alongside the tools that support it. The printing press carried stories across continents; typewriters and computers refined how we shape them. Today, artificial intelligence is simply the newest instrument in that lineage—not a replacement for imagination, but an extension of it.

AI helps organize and articulate ideas that originate in the writer's mind and heart. Some argue that its use makes a book less authentic. In truth, it can make storytelling more accessible; anyone with a story—a parent, a dreamer, a traveler, a thinker—can now bring it to life. AI is a bridge between inspiration and expression.

Transparency Note

At its core, *Ocean Earth* grew out of my personal lived experiences—war, helplessness, fear, family, separation, longing, hope, and coming home. Every scene, theme, and character arc began from that human foundation. For deeper insight into the personal story behind the novel, kindly read the **Author's Note: "The Human Behind the Story"** at the end of the book.

As this is my debut work, shaping the novel into its final form involved thousands of pages of instructions, experiments, revisions, and creative exchanges with AI tools that helped me translate my vision into the story it became. For readers interested in how this human–AI collaboration brought *Ocean Earth* to life, I am planning a companion volume that reveals the extensive process behind the scenes.

Ocean Earth Saga

Book I — *Ocean Earth (Until Next Time)*: A father and son cross a drowned world to find the family they fear the flood has taken.

Sequel I — *The Long Road Home (Through the Far East)*: Exploration of Asia's reborn civilizations—new alliances, rogue powers, hostile nature, and a quest to balance technology with humility.

Sequel II — *Mars Is Calling*. Humanity looks upward once again, building the first interplanetary civilization, and carrying Earth's lessons into a new world.

Conceptual Highlights

Several imaginative ideas appear throughout *Ocean Earth*, briefly referenced in conversation, reflection, or metaphor. They are not formal scientific claims, but thought experiments the characters use to make sense of a transforming world.

For readers who wish to explore these concepts beyond their role in the story, see **"Homemade Science"** near the end of this book.

- The Universe Cake Concept
- Orientation of Our World
- Consciousness Is the Fifth Dimension, and Life Is a Force
- The Black Hole Medium
- $E = mc^2$ at Equilibrium
- Twisting and Untwisting Space
- Observation, Waves, and the Medium of Reality
- Instantaneity and the Center
- Homemade Science

Contents

The Anomaly 1

Reality Setting In 7

Dark Water Ahead 15

The Fly-Through 31

Ocean Earth 51

The Search for the Lost 67

The Real and the Imaginary 87

New New York 95

The Great Crossing 113

Why the Journey? 129

New Europe 143

Heading East 159

The Return... 179

The Anomaly

The observatory stood like a cathedral of silence. Only the cooling system's low hum and the telescope's steady metallic clicks disturbed the stillness as it pivoted toward another sector of sky. Sam Saphire sat alone at the console, eyes fixed on the monitor. Rows of numbers flickered across the screen—starlight translated into data. To anyone else, meaningless; to him, a story waiting to be understood.

Tonight, the story refused to cohere. He leaned closer, zooming in on a faint streak barely etched across the star field. At first, he dismissed it—noise, interference. But the subsequent exposure returned it, more precise and sharper. Not a star. Not a galaxy. Something else. Rubbing his eyes, he reached for the cold coffee he'd abandoned hours ago and swallowed the bitterness. *Another comet,* he told himself. *Hundreds are cataloged every year.* But the arc's curve gnawed at him.

He powered off the last monitor. Afterimages of graphs and shifting star fields danced in his tired vision. When the equipment fell silent, the weight of discovery—or of a huge mistake—settled heavily across his shoulders. He gathered his notes, slid them into his worn leather satchel, and stepped into the night.

The drive home was quiet—the kind that amplified thought. Streetlights thinned, shadows deepened. The house looked warm, familiar, ordinary, but Sam knew nothing would stay ordinary for long.

Inside, the scent of brewed tea lingered in the air, the hall clock ticking softly. He set the satchel on the kitchen table, sank into a chair, and stared into nothing, rehearsing explanations he wasn't sure he could give. Then he rose, went straight to his home office, switched on the computer, and plunged back into files, graphs, and data.

Before long, the door opened gently. Eisha stepped inside, robe wrapped around her, hair loose over her shoulders, concern and weary patience in her eyes.

"Sam," she murmured. "It's nearly three. Why don't you come to bed?"

He didn't look away from the screen. "I know. I just … need to finish these runs."

She came to his side, resting a hand on his shoulder. "What is it that's keeping you up?"

He gestured at the monitor. "That faint light. Here—see it?"

She leaned in. "Barely. Another comet?"

"Maybe," he said slowly. "That's the easy answer."

"But you don't think so."

He hesitated. "It doesn't behave like one. Comets come in, brighten under solar warmth, then slingshot away. This … doesn't fit. It's almost as if…" His voice drifted off.

"As if what?" she pressed gently.

"As if we're moving *toward* it. Which shouldn't happen—not like this."

Eisha frowned. "So, what else could it be?"

Sam leaned back, dragging a hand over his face. "Dust cloud. Ice fragments. Uncharted debris… Space is full of surprises."

"Surprises," she echoed, her voice tight. "Not very comforting."

He tried to smile. It didn't reach his eyes. "It isn't. But I need more data before I jump to conclusions."

She studied him in the glow of the monitor. The light carved deeper lines around his eyes, darker shadows beneath. "Sam," she said quietly, "promise me something. Whatever this is—don't carry it alone. If it matters, you'll need others. Don't try to solve the universe by yourself."

Her words sank in. He nodded, distracted. The streak on his screen wouldn't fade. Neither would the feeling in his chest.

***

Two weeks later, in the institute's research wing, Sam met with the two colleagues he trusted most. Jian Wu, orbital mechanics expert with a razor-sharp mind, stood with arms crossed, eyes fixed on the screen. Beside him, Dr. Alana Reyes adjusted her glasses, her concern deepening.

Sam walked them through the data—exposure after exposure, simulations overlaid on the solar system. "At first, I thought it was a comet," he began. "But the trajectory doesn't fit. It's not approaching us. The solar system is drifting into it."

Alana leaned forward. "Into what, exactly?"

Sam took a breath. "I didn't want to come to you with just my data. In the last two weeks, I've contacted observatories in Chile and Hawaii, as well as the orbital array. They all ran sweeps on the coordinates. Everyone confirmed the anomaly."

He tapped a sequence of keys. Spectral graphs appeared beside telescope imagery. "Signatures are consistent across instruments—strong blue and ultraviolet reflection. Frozen water. Not dust. Not rock. Ice. A massive region of it."

He highlighted a faint arc. "This isn't a single body. It's a belt—millions of kilometers wide. And in under two years, the solar system will pass right through it. Invisible until now, but it's revealing itself as we drift closer."

Silence stretched. Jian finally broke it. "A belt that wide... Catastrophic."

Alana's voice stayed calm, though heavy. "This isn't just some meteor shower. Earth is entering an environment it was never meant to encounter."

Sam nodded grimly. "Ice fragments. Some will burn up in the atmosphere. Many won't. Oceans rise. Weather spirals. Flooding, storms—possibly much worse."

Jian rubbed his forehead. "Gaia Archive? Kepler...?"

"Three checks," Sam answered. "Independent confirmation last night. The belt is real."

Alana sat back as the truth settled over them. "Sam, this isn't something you keep private. The world needs to know. Take it to the government."

He shook his head. "The models are incomplete. What if we sound the alarm, and it's nothing?"

Jian's expression sharpened. "And what if it's everything, and we waste time?"

Sam had no answer. His mouth went dry.

That night, Eisha found him pacing the living room. The kids' schoolbooks lay scattered across the coffee table, Sarah's science project on the solar system beaming from a paper—bright sun, lopsided planets.

"They're asleep?" Sam asked quietly.

"Out cold," she said, studying him. "You look ten years older."

He sank onto the couch. "Jian and Alana confirmed it. It's not a comet. It's real. Worse than I expected."

She sat beside him, waiting.

"They want me to go to Washington," he said. "The president."

Her hand closed over his. "And you don't want to?"

He shook his head. "Once I do, there's no rewind. Panic. Headlines. Governments scrambling. And if we can't stop it…"

Eisha held his gaze, steady as stone. "Sam, isn't that why you speak? If it's real, the world deserves every second to prepare."

He stared at her. Her calm anchored him even as fear twisted inside. She was right. She always was.

His chest tightened again—a physical ache. He pressed a fist to his sternum, forcing the emotion down.

***

The next evening, Sam stood once more in the observatory. Jian and Alana hovered behind him as fresh readings scrolled across the monitors.

"Trajectory confirmed," Jian said. "Intersection in approximately two years."

Alana turned to Sam. "No more hesitation. You know what comes next."

Sam swallowed, eyes locked on the faint ice-gleam in the void. His hand trembled as he reached for the phone.

"I'll reach out to Washington," he said softly.

For the first time, the stars filled him not with wonder ... but with dread.

Reality Setting In

The West Wing briefing room carried the scent of burnt coffee and warm printer ink, an aroma baked into its walls after decades of crises. President James Landers sat at the head of the long oak table, fingers tapping a restless rhythm. Staffers moved with quiet precision, sliding folders and tablets into place as if assembling a machine bracing for overload. Screens flickered to life along the walls, washing the room in pale blue.

A red light glowed on the secure line.

"Your Cabinet's here, sir," the chief of staff informed the president. "Dr. Saphire is on line two."

Landers inhaled. "Let them in."

The double doors opened. Secretaries, defense analysts, economists, and scientists entered with tense postures, anticipating bad news. Chairs scraped. Pages rustled. Solar maps and spectral models rippled across the screens.

Landers initiated the conference feed. "Mr. Saphire."

Sam's calm voice filled the room. "Good morning, Mr. President. Good morning, everyone."

"Give us the summary," Landers said, clipped but steady.

"A few weeks ago, I spotted what looked like a comet," Sam began. "But its behavior wasn't consistent with a typical orbit. To confirm, I reached out to observatories in Chile, Hawaii, South Africa, and the orbital array. Independent instruments. Multiple angles. All results matched."

He paused.

"The object isn't approaching us," Sam said. "We're drifting into something—an ancient, previously undetectable belt of ice."

Landers leaned forward. "Drifting into *what*, exactly?"

"Ice," Sam repeated. "Layered. Fractured. Possibly embedded with objects we hope are not asteroids."

A Cabinet member frowned. "What's the difference?"

"Ice burns and shatters. Asteroids don't. Ice brings destruction. Rock brings annihilation."

Unease rippled around the table.

Landers's jaw tightened. "So, what do we do?"

"Prepare for water," Sam said. "A lot of it."

The room froze. Even the ventilation seemed to soften.

"Time frame?" Landers asked.

"Right now, roughly two years before major impacts begin. We must prepare for a hydrological event unlike anything in human history."

Alarmed murmurs followed.

When the call ended, no one rose. It felt as if standing might tip the world further off balance.

"Everyone wants the answer to the same question," Landers said quietly. "What next?"

Later that evening, Landers entered the Oval Office. The room felt unusually still, as though listening.

"Pam," he said to his aide, "get me Governor Jay Peters on Mars."

She blinked. "Mars, sir?"

"Mars."

She obeyed, dialing the secure interplanetary line.

"Mr. President?" Governor Peters's voice crackled through.

"How are things on Mars?" Landers asked.

"Dry, cold, and thin," Peters replied. "Standard conditions."

"Not for long," Landers said. "Ice is coming your way."

Peters didn't sound surprised. "Our polar satellites caught reflectivity patterns. Layered. Primordial. Not a comet—an environment."

"So, your timeline?" Landers pressed.

"Roughly two years. Maybe earlier waves. Our atmosphere will burn up less of it than yours."

Landers exhaled. "We need full coordination—your scientists and ours. Earth and Mars now face the same storm. Two planets, one survival clock."

"Understood," Peters said.

The call ended. The Oval Office felt colder for it.

***

On Mars, thin winds curled around steel-and-glass domes. The red planet stirred under the same cosmic tide. Governor Peters leaned back in his chair, staring at Mars' golden haze through his pod's window. He imagined Earth turning beneath the same threat, unaware that fragments might already be brushing its upper atmosphere.

If Earth fell, Mars inherited its burden.

If Mars faltered, humanity shrank to a memory.

Two worlds. One countdown. One approaching storm.

***

Back on Earth, Sam sat alone in his office, lit only by shifting simulations. Each new model was worse than the last. He rubbed his eyes, haunted by the Cabinet's expressions—fear disguised as formality, resolve stitched to desperation.

He thought of his children, their science projects on galaxies, stars, and distant worlds.

He thought, "We're running out of time."

***

Within days, the media seized on whispers of the president's briefings—and on a more startling leak: the president had spoken directly with officials on Mars. By morning, every major network displayed split screens of Sam Saphire and swirling animations of cosmic ice.

Morning shows filled their couches with physicists, theologians, economists, climate experts, and inevitable doomsday preppers. Predictions multiplied like sparks in dry brush. Some claimed the event might be akin to a cosmic snowfall—harmless, even beautiful. Others spoke bluntly of extinction-level flooding.

That night, Sam and Eisha sat on the couch. The TV was muted. The lamp glowed softly. Adam and Sarah were working on homework, unaware of the storm the world was sliding toward.

"Dad?" Adam said.

Sam turned, exhaustion easing into curiosity. "What is it?"

"I've been thinking about the universe," Adam said. "I have a theory."

Sam managed to smile. "A theory, huh? Let's hear it."

"I think the universe is like a cake."

Sam chuckled. "The Universe Cake Theory?"

Adam nodded earnestly. "Yeah. In one state, you have ingredients—space, time, matter, energy. Like sugar, flour, eggs. In another, you have the cake—like a black hole. It's a giant space-batter mixer."

Sam leaned forward, intrigued. "Go on."

"I think science uses the wrong words sometimes," Adam continued. "Once you're outside our 'ingredient universe,' our vocabulary stops working. That's why certain experiments look impossible."

"Like which ones?" Sam asked.

"The double-slit experiment. Quantum entanglement. Black holes… Maybe they only seem hard to explain because we're trying to read cake recipes with ingredient eyes."

Eisha smirked. "Interesting."

Adam shrugged. "It's like studying cake with ingredient-universe tools—or like looking at yourself in a fun house mirror."

"Any constants in your theory?" Sam prompted.

Adam hesitated. "Consciousness. If consciousness doesn't exist, nothing else exists. Without it, even the idea of existence disappears."

Sam stared—speechless, overwhelmed, proud.

"Clear as mud," he quipped.

Adam grinned. They laughed together. For a moment, cosmic ice belts and political chaos faded into the background under the warmth of home.

***

Later that week, President Landers sat alone in the Oval Office. Headlines—*DOOM OR DELUSION?*—echoed in his mind.

"Pam," he said, "clear the room. I need to make a call."

"To who, sir?"

"The Pope."

"… The Pope?"

"Yes, Pam. The Pope." He sighed. "My Cabinet thinks I'm insane anyway. My opponents will have a field day. But I am interested to hear his perspective."

Moments later, a warm voice filled the secure line.

"Good afternoon, Mr. President. Or is it morning there?"

"Still morning," Landers replied. "You've seen the news?"

"I have," the Pope said gently. "Troubling developments, indeed."

"What do you think?" Landers asked.

"Another flood?" the Pope said softly. "Only God knows."

"Is this how the first flood happened?" Landers pressed. "Where did all that water come from—and go?"

"God created the universe," the Pope said simply. "Creating water—or withdrawing it—would not be difficult for Him."

"So, why allow this at all?"

"Is this a moment of religious awakening?" the Pope asked.

"I'm ... asking for a friend."

"The Son of God suffered in this world," the Pope replied. "It was never meant to be paradise. Yet we are given good days—mercies we do not earn."

Landers let out a small laugh. "So, we're lucky to even have the good days?"

"You catch on quickly," the Pope said warmly. "Good luck, Mr. President. And goodbye."

The line clicked off.

Landers stared at the receiver for a moment too long.

"Pam," he called, "should I call the Dalai Lama next?"

Pam folded her arms. "They all know about the flood," she said. "You'd think they'd all been there."

Landers didn't respond. Something had settled over him. Not fear. Acceptance.

Reality had finally set in.

Dark Water Ahead

The news continued to spread faster than fear itself. What began as a quiet hum in academic circles—Sam Saphire's strange data about an approaching cosmic mass—had grown into a global drumbeat. Every home glowed with televisions replaying the same updates; every radio whispered warnings; every conversation bent toward the same looming reality. Within weeks, the world had stopped pretending life was normal.

Sam felt it most clearly each night when he returned home. Windows along the street flickered with news channels. Neighbors stood in their driveways, arguing over evacuation plans or water purification kits. Even the air felt different, thick with anticipation.

At dinner, the silence cracked first under Eisha's steady voice. She folded her napkin with deliberate calm.

"Sam," she said, "what exactly are we supposed to prepare for? Are we talking about storms? Floods? Something worse?"

Sam exhaled slowly. "Every nation, every family needs to plan for a global flood. We don't know how high it could get. But we have to assume it could be extreme."

Sarah frowned. "But Dad, if you don't know, how do we know what's going to happen?"

"We plan for the middle," Sam said. "Not nothing, but not total extinction. Some cities will vanish. Some land will survive. Preparation is what separates survival from devastation."

Eisha tapped her fork against her plate nervously, the sound sharp in the quiet room. "So, what does preparation look like? For regular families?"

Sam spread his hands. "We build things that float. Stockpile food. Learn to live on water. For a while, humanity may have to become an aquatic species."

The table fell into a heavy silence.

Adam pushed his chair back and stood abruptly. His face had gone pale. Without a word, he slipped out of the kitchen. Sarah watched him go, worry clear in her expression. After a moment, she followed.

She found her brother sitting on the edge of his bed, elbows on his knees, staring at the floor.

"Adam?" she said softly.

He hesitated, then looked up. "You know Rachelle, right? From across the street?"

Sarah snorted. "Everyone knows you're obsessed with her."

He blinked. "I didn't think it was that obvious."

"It is. You're like a sunflower tracking the sun every time she walks outside."

He gave a weak smile, but it faded quickly. "I always thought I'd get to talk to her someday. Maybe see her in college—maybe more. Now I'm wondering if I'll ever see her again. Or if anyone will."

Sarah sat beside him. "You're seventeen. You're moving away to go to college soon. There will be other girls."

"Maybe," he murmured. "But it feels like the world is about to steal a chance I didn't even get to take."

She leaned her head gently against his shoulder. "That's not love, Adam. That's longing. And longing is ... tricky."

He chuckled faintly. "Maybe when I finally meet her, I'll realize I was lucky the ocean kept her away."

Their soft laughter eased the tension. But it didn't erase it.

A knock sounded on the doorframe. Sam stepped in.

"You two okay?" he asked.

"Just talking about people we'd miss," Sarah said.

Sam looked at Adam. "Anyone in particular?"

Adam swallowed. "Honestly? You all. I love our life. Breakfast together, school one mile away, familiar neighborhood, evenings at home, a full house, barbecues with friends and family, Mom cooking... I don't want it to change. I don't want to lose anyone."

Sam nodded slowly. "That fear means you care. Hold onto that."

Eisha appeared next, wiping her hands on a dishtowel. "What's all this heavy talk?" she asked.

Sarah sighed. "Just thinking about what happens if we get separated."

Eisha sat down beside them. "Then we face it like people before us did. Look at history—wars, disasters, families torn apart overnight. People didn't choose it. But they endured. And those who survived ... built life again."

Sam listened quietly as she spoke.

17

"If it's too big to stop," Eisha continued, "we can't control it. But if it's something we can beat, we'll beat it together. Either way, we don't let fear decide who we become."

Sarah nodded slowly.

Eisha shifted to lighter territory. "And what about Sean? That Australian kid who helps out at the marina?"

Sarah rolled her eyes. "He's great. But I don't feel … that spark."

Sam smiled. "Feelings aren't a checklist."

Adam raised an eyebrow. "What if Rachelle doesn't feel anything for me?"

Eisha touched his shoulder gently. "Attraction isn't owed. You put your truth out there. If it's returned, good. If not, it still matters that you felt it."

"The truest kind of love," Sam said, "is when you feel it with every atom of your being—and then discover that the other person feels it just as deeply. When that happens, it's a gift. Until then … it's infatuation."

Before the mood got too heavy again, Eisha stood and declared, "All right. Enough apocalyptic romance for one night." She kissed their heads and left the room.

Later, when Sam and Eisha sat alone, she curled into the corner of the couch, arms wrapped around her knees. The television glowed silently, scrolling government advisories across the bottom of the screen.

Eisha's voice cracked. "Sam … I can't stop picturing the kids lost somewhere. Drifting. Calling for us. What if we can't find them?"

Sam reached for her hand. "That's why we plan ahead."

"What plan?" she asked softly. "We don't control the ocean. Or luck."

He took a breath. "Adam's graduating next month. The college nearby sits on high ground. Strong infrastructure. It'll be one of the safest places in the city. We'll keep both kids there—Adam starting classes, Sarah dual-enrolling. We stay close, no matter what."

"And if things collapse sooner?"

"Then we adapt." He squeezed her hand. "Dean Rivers is creating a preparedness group. Sean's joining. They're retrofitting the campus—solar, water, communications. We'll coordinate with them."

Eisha's eyes softened. "You've thought about this."

"I'm trying to keep us safe," he said. "We'll also have alternate meet-up points and radios. Layers of protection." He hesitated. "And I talked to my family overseas."

Eisha straightened. "Are they okay?"

"They're preparing. I told them to move to our old mountain town, nine hundred meters above sea level. If the water ever reaches that height…" He paused. "Well. None of us will be around to argue."

Eisha managed a brittle smile. "Maybe we should move there, too."

"Maybe." He kissed her forehead. "But wherever we are, we'll face it together."

A distant rumble of thunder rolled through the neighborhood. Lights flickered. Outside, neighbors hammered boards onto small rafts or tested generators in their driveways. The world was already changing.

Inside, the family stayed close, sharing the quiet as if it were sacred.

For one moment, ordinary life held.

***

The following weekend, the community center filled up long before the meeting began. Folding chairs scraped across the hardwood floor as neighbors rushed to claim seats. Children clung to their parents' hands. The smell of coffee and damp coats lingered in the air. People were scared, but even more, they were desperate to understand.

Sam stepped to the front of the room. Not as a scientist behind a podium, but as someone who lived two streets over, someone whose kids had played with theirs, someone who had studied the anomaly longer than anyone else in the building. He held the microphone, scanning the worried faces.

"Thank you for coming," he began. "I know everyone wants clarity, and none of us has enough of it yet. But here's what we do know."

He paused, choosing the image carefully—not to frighten, but to make the truth unavoidable.

"I want you to picture the Empire State Building."

The room stilled.

"Now imagine the ocean rising high enough to cover it."

Gasps rippled through the hall. Someone whispered a prayer. A few people shook their heads in disbelief, but no one laughed. No one denied it anymore.

"If sea levels rise by three hundred to four hundred meters," Sam continued, "nearly every major coastal city on Earth will disappear. That means billions displaced. But displacement isn't the same as extinction. We only reach extinction if we fail to prepare."

Hands shot up all at once.

"What about food?" someone asked.

"We start thinking like sailors—and like farmers at sea," Sam said. "We build floating communities that work the way farms do: everyone contributes, everyone eats. We store what we can, learn to fish, learn to purify water, and we practice living on the water before we're forced to."

"What about storms?" a woman called from the back.

"Then we stay together," Sam replied. "It's hard to survive alone at sea. Communities that cooperate will make it. People who drift off on their own … may not."

Concerned murmurs filled the room.

"We'll also need clear meeting points," Sam added. "Places on the map everyone knows. A fallback plan for when phones and satellites fail. 'If we're separated, we regroup at Point A'—simple decisions like that save lives."

People were nodding now—slowly, reluctantly, but they were hearing him. Accepting that preparation was no longer paranoia. It was survival.

Sam set down the microphone.

Neighbors lingered long after the meeting ended. Old grievances over fences, noise, or parking evaporated under a new shared purpose. People exchanged phone numbers. They discussed rafts, supplies, and tools. Some offered workshops on fishing knots. Others volunteered to help repair outboard motors.

Humanity, Sam realized, didn't fall apart first. It pulled itself together.

The falling apart came later.

***

Two days later, the entire nation turned to their screens as the White House press briefing went live. President Landers stood at the podium, flanked by military advisors, FEMA officials, and scientists in crisp suits. His jaw was tight. His hands gripped the podium as if he were holding the country itself in place.

"My fellow Americans," he began, "we can no longer treat this as a distant threat. We must treat it as certain. The issue isn't if Earth will be affected, but how much, and whether we'll be ready."

Behind him, the screen lit up with seven stark bullet points—no commentary, no softening, just reality.

1. Reallocation of manufacturing to boats, floating platforms, and emergency watercraft.

Factories were already receiving new orders; industries were shifting overnight.

2. Establishment of emergency reserves in mountain depots.

Food, medicine, seeds, generators—everything essential was being stockpiled where floodwaters could never reach.

3. Fast-track development of amphibious aircraft.

Planes that could take off from and land on water, replacing traditional airports.

4. Expansion of short-range drone programs for local transport.

Single-person and family-size drones designed to hop between rising islands and floating towns.

5. Deployment of buoyed communication towers.

Floating antenna structures, anchored deep into the seabed, meant to preserve satellite links for as long as possible.

6. Preservation of global knowledge in waterproof mountain vaults.

Humanity's books, films, science, and cultural memory—sealed away in digital form.

7. Mandatory family survival kits.

Life vests. Desalination canteens. Radios. Solar chargers. Compasses. Basic tools. And—to the discomfort of many—means of self-defense.

The president gave that final point a heavy pause.

"We will not pretend humanity is at its best in times of desperation. Families must be prepared to protect what keeps them alive."

The reporters in the room didn't shout or argue. No one had the energy for denial anymore.

The briefing ended, and every news channel in the world cut to analysis. But none captured the tone as sharply as World News Network. The anchor, a silver-haired woman known for her unshakable calm, leaned toward the camera.

"Ladies and gentlemen," she said, "the United States government has just confirmed what scientists have hinted at: we are preparing not only for global disaster, but for a transformation of human civilization."

Behind her, animations displayed the future. Seaplanes skimming waves instead of landing on runways. Drones flying across flooded suburbs. Buoyed towers rising like metal sentinels above endless water. Waterproof digital vaults sealed into mountain caverns.

"This is not a temporary disruption," the anchor continued. "This is a shift in how humanity will live."

A new graphic appeared, a simple message stretching across the screen:

PREPARE FOR A WORLD OF WATER.

PREPARE AS IF SURVIVAL DEPENDS ON IT.

Out in the suburbs, people stopped pretending they didn't see the writing on the wall. Hardware stores sold out of rope, patch kits, and small solar panels. Carpenters offered lessons in waterproofing. Teenagers practiced tying knots in their garages.

In Sam's neighborhood, the shift was visible. Children tested life vests in backyard pools. Neighbors dragged old rowboats into their garages to repair seams. Radios crackled with emergency frequencies as families tested channels and call signs.

The country had not yet reached the moment when land would drown, and seas would rise. But it had reached the moment when everyone understood: life had already changed.

That night, Sam stepped outside to the driveway, looking up at the sky. It was clear, cloudless, deceptively calm. Across the street, two neighbors were building a raft with old barrels. Down the block, someone tested a small generator. The low hum carried through the cool air like a warning.

He thought back to the town hall, to the White House briefing, to the tremor in Eisha's voice when she feared losing the children. All of it was pushing in the same direction. The world was shifting beneath their feet—not slowly, but with gathering speed.

Humanity was beginning to prepare. Really prepare. But deep down, Sam knew the truth no one wanted to say out loud. Preparation wasn't an end. It was just the beginning.

***

While neighborhoods patched rafts and governments repurposed factories, the rest of the planet lurched into its own race against the clock. Every country responded differently—some with ingenuity, some with desperation, all with urgency.

In Tokyo, engineers had begun fastening enormous buoyant platforms around the bases of skyscrapers—floating decks built to rise with the water, lifting entire districts a few meters at a time. As the sea climbed, these platforms would turn each tower into a hybrid structure: a floating city hub with a building at its center, its lower fortified floors still usable beneath the surface. Crowds watched from the sidewalks—half in awe, half in dread.

In Lagos, families lashed oil drums and bamboo into makeshift flotillas. Children carried buckets of nails, while fathers hammered long after sundown. Churches urged people to store not just food, but faith.

In the Swiss Alps, steel containers swung beneath military helicopters into icy valleys. Seeds, medicines, batteries, and solar panels filled the new mountain vaults, quiet bunkers becoming strongholds for the world's memory.

In Sydney, surfers stood at the coastline as waves crashed against seawalls already pressed tight against the city's edge. Shipyards worked around the clock, transforming ferries into floating neighborhoods with solar roofs and reinforced hulls.

And across the world, shipyards and factories roared back to life under new blueprints. Car plants stamped out modular pontoons. Ships became drifting cities. Farmers relocated their farms to higher ground, choosing whatever land might stay dry, hoping the coming water would spare it.

Everywhere, the same truth echoed: Earth was not just preparing for a disaster. Earth was preparing to become something new.

***

Far above the planet, another plan was unfolding—bolder, stranger, and perhaps even more desperate.

The Mars Contingency Program had been activated.

For years, it had been no more than a quiet conversation in government backrooms. Now, it had become a relentless mission, swallowing budgets, manpower, and launch windows. Rocket engines rumbled day and night across Florida, Kazakhstan, French Guiana, and China. The skies never stayed dark for long; another plume of fire always lit the horizon. Payloads varied, but shared a single intention: ensure that humanity survived somewhere.

Some ships carried scientists—experts in agriculture, medicine, engineering, and communications. Some carried government envoys, intended to be the first seeds of an administration in exile. Others carried cryogenic vaults—seeds, DNA samples, embryos, archives. The rest were filled with infrastructure—solar collectors, atmospheric processors, tools, and materials. Each launch was a page in a last-minute manual for saving a species.

Sam watched many of the launches on television late at night. News anchors called it the Great Shuttle Era, showing time-lapsed footage of rockets arcing into the sky like burning arrows. Children around the world pointed upward into the night, searching for the faint line of moving stars.

But Sam understood something unspoken: Mars wasn't just a backup for Earth. Mars also depended on Earth more than anyone admitted. If the anomaly damaged both planets, each world would become the other's lifeline.

Governor Jay Peters's relationship with President Landers balanced somewhere between respect and rivalry. Earth had once tried to sideline him. But now? He was indispensable. And without Earth's constant supply chain, Mars couldn't sustain the population it already had. Two planets—once separated by politics and pride—were now tied at the throat.

One evening, Eisha joined Sam on the couch as another launch thundered across the TV.

"Does it help," she asked quietly, "knowing that … someone out there might carry on?"

Sam thought about it for a long moment. "It helps that we're trying. It scares me that we have to."

"And if Mars ends up being all that's left?"

Sam shook his head. "I don't know if it'll still feel like us."

Eisha rested her hand on his. "Better something different than nothing at all."

***

Months passed. The world shifted again. This time, it was not with chaos, but with a strange settling.

People adapted to the nonstop Armageddon news. The urgency that once electrified every conversation dulled into routine. Preparations continued, but with less adrenaline and more resignation. Humanity had grown used to waiting for a disaster it could not see.

Adam left for college first, just as he'd planned months earlier, though the uncertainty of everything ahead muted his excitement. A year later, Sarah followed—determined, anxious, hopeful. Sam and Eisha watched them both go, reviewing the family emergency plan each time: rendezvous points, backup communication, a promise to find one another no matter what came.

When the kids were gone, the house felt both too quiet and too normal. The world hadn't ended. Life hadn't stopped. It had simply ... adapted.

At the university, Adam sent messages describing the uneasy atmosphere—sirens tested more often, emergency posters everywhere, students whispering about timelines and worst-case scenarios between lectures. Sarah found the campus the same: life carrying on, but the ground beneath it subtly trembling.

Back home, entire industries had reinvented themselves. Car manufacturers became boat builders. Airlines became seaplane companies. Delivery companies became drone fleets. Telecom giants raced to anchor buoyed towers across oceans, so satellites wouldn't fall silent. Schools held life-vest drills instead of active-shooter drills. Churches added desalination to their community courses. Garages filled with tools, rope, barrels, and welding sparks. Neighborhoods talked through flotilla scenarios—who had boats, which rafts could tow neighbors, where people might gather if roads became waterways.

The world was not sinking … yet. But the world was already floating.

One night, after the neighborhood grew quiet, Sam stood at the window. Lights glowed in garages where people were tightening bolts on makeshift pontoons or testing emergency radios. The faint hum of a generator drifted through the cool air.

The phone on the table buzzed sharply. Sam froze. He already knew who it was.

He picked up.

"Dr. Saphire?" a crisp voice said. "This is the White House."

A short pause.

"The president needs you—immediately."

Sam felt his pulse quicken.

The world was no longer just preparing around him. Now he was being pulled into the center of it.

The Fly-Through

Sam was already on the line with the White House when the world began to look upward.

"Sir, we're getting reports from six continents," a voice said through the secure channel. "People are calling emergency lines, news stations, churches—everywhere."

Sam moved to the window. Even from here, he could see them.

The sky had erupted into pale, luminous arcs—long white streaks suspended across the heavens, glowing where the sun caught them just right. They hung there in impossible stillness, like brushstrokes that refused to fade. If you didn't know better, you could mistake them for angels—angels bearing a message of peace, even though the angel of the end of times was said to arrive with a sword of fire.

And that was the problem. The beauty was disarming. The stillness was a lie.

Across the neighborhood, people had come outside—some with phones raised to capture the event, some whispering, some crying. A few knelt in driveways, convinced they were witnessing a sign from heaven. Others clutched each other, trembling. One woman pressed her palms together, praying softly as if the sky might answer.

But the "angels" were nothing of the kind. They were the first visible crest of the incoming belt, illuminated ice fragments racing toward them faster than the mind could comprehend—moving so quickly that they seemed motionless. The spectacle was breathtaking, but it was a breathless kind of beauty—the kind that arrives before something breaks.

"Still nothing from the ocean monitoring network?" Sam asked.

"Not exactly," the voice replied. "Several fragments entered over open water. They superheated, broke apart on descent, and turned into massive amounts of vapor—came down as sheets of rain."

Sam's stomach tightened.

Rain, not shock waves. Water from above—not the rising tsunami walls of ocean everyone feared from below. A slight relief—yet somehow even more unsettling.

"That's why the president wants you here," the voice continued. "He needs to understand what these initial impacts are telling us—and what we can tell the public."

Outside his window, the street was still filling with people—some pointing upward in awe, others backing away in fear. Somewhere down the block, a car alarm went off, then stopped abruptly. The world felt both louder and quieter than it should have, as if sound itself were bracing for whatever would come next.

Sam grabbed his coat. "Tell the president I'm on my way."

***

Inside the West Wing, the Situation Room buzzed with controlled urgency. The president stood at the head of the table, flanked by the directors of NASA, NOAA, the USGS, and Joint Space Command. Screens along the walls displayed global radar sweeps, atmospheric models, and looping simulations of the belt thickening—an expanding halo of debris creeping toward Earth's orbit like frost spreading across glass.

Sam took his seat as the president addressed the room.

"All right," President Landers said, voice steady but strained. "We need clarity. What exactly are we dealing with?"

A NASA physicist gestured to a display showing a fragment's atmospheric entry. "We believe these objects are composed almost entirely of volatile ices—spectral data indicates water ice. Their structure collapses on entry. They vaporize before reaching the ground."

The NOAA director nodded. "That vapor cools rapidly and condenses. The result is rainfall—intense, yes, but not explosive. No tsunamis. No mega-shocks. The ocean absorbs it."

Another scientist added, "We may see extreme sea level rise, regionally severe flooding, but catastrophic asteroid-like impacts seem unlikely."

Sam rested his hands on the table. "Unlikely doesn't mean impossible. And the models are only as good as the assumptions we put in."

The room fell quiet.

"We're watching," the president said finally, "and so far, the impacts have ... softened. Dissolved. Turned into rain. That's the data we have."

His expression flickered, just for a moment, with doubt—a wince or a worry Sam couldn't quite read.

Sam hesitated. "Rain can drown a world, too. Slowly. Quietly. In ways people won't recognize until it's too late."

Several in the room nodded, yet the lowered odds of catastrophic impact had diluted the sense of urgency. The mood leaned toward relief. Measured. Controlled. Almost hopeful.

And outside these walls, Sam thought, *the world is clinging to any hint of reassurance—true or not.*

The president exhaled. "For now, we tell the public the truth: the immediate catastrophic danger appears low. We prepare, but we don't panic the world."

Sam wasn't sure that was the truth—but the alternative wasn't clear either. Not yet.

He stepped out of the Situation Room into the corridor as his phone buzzed with notifications, news clips, social feeds, and messages from his kids. The world was reacting.

In bars, talk shows, and online echo chambers, the skeptics mounted their counterattack.

"Nothing's happening," one red-faced pundit scoffed on a live broadcast. "Weeks of fearmongering. Billions—maybe trillions—wasted worldwide. Scientists spreading panic just to obtain funding."

Another chimed in. "Fear is the most profitable commodity there is. The elites want you to be terrified. They want you to buy boats and hoard food while they fly off to Mars."

The studio audience applauded. Memes mocked "Dr. Doom Saphire." Hashtags multiplied: #IceScam, #NothingBurger, #LetUsLive, #HailHydroFreeze.

Sam saw it all. He wasn't immune to the noise. His kids saw the memes, too.

"Dad ... what if they're right?" Sarah had asked with a shaky laugh that wasn't quite a laugh at all.

Even Sam's neighbors looked torn—half preparing, half in denial. One family had parked a brand-new amphibious ATV in their driveway. Another scrubbed their grill for a cookout as if nothing unusual were happening.

For the moment, the oceans swallowed the ice quietly, and the world, desperate for normalcy, latched onto the illusion. It was easier to believe nothing would happen than to prepare for the worst.

But beneath that uneasy calm, the clock ticked relentlessly. The belt was thickening. The real storm had not yet begun.

That night, Sam's house held its breath. The living room television was dark. Radios sat quietly on shelves. Even the usual hum of the home felt different, as though the walls themselves sensed a shift in the world beyond them.

Around the dinner table, plates sat untouched. The air felt charged—not like fear, exactly, but like awareness. Forks tapped porcelain in a slow, irregular rhythm.

It was Sarah who broke the hush.

"Dad," she said, her voice soft but steady, "I have a theory."

Sam looked up from his untouched plate. "I'm listening."

Sarah leaned forward, her fingers tracing slow circles on the table's surface. Her eyes glimmered with that mix of curiosity and boldness he'd always admired in her.

"Since the solar system is traveling through the universe in a certain direction," she began, "doesn't that mean, for us, there's a front and back? Maybe even an up and down? Defined by that motion?"

Sam smiled faintly. "It's all relative. But in principle, the North Pole is roughly aligned with the ecliptic—the plane of our solar system's motion. So, yes, in a poetic sense, it could be considered the front or up, and the South Pole the down or back."

Sarah's face lit up with triumph. "Exactly."

Sam squinted at her. "Are you preparing to argue with your Australian ex again?"

Sarah's grin widened. "You know it."Even Eisha cracked a small, reluctant smile.

Laughter drifted around the table, thinning the tension like a sudden breeze. For a moment, the world outside felt distant, manageable, less monstrous.

Sam turned to Adam. "All right—your turn. Got another theory for us?"

Adam dabbed his mouth with a napkin in exaggerated seriousness. "Actually, yes. I've been thinking about dimensions."

Sam sighed and leaned back. "Of course you have."

Adam's grin widened. "Hear me out. Everyone accepts space and time. Four dimensions—standard stuff. But I think the next dimension isn't something mathematical or invisible. I think the fifth dimension is consciousness. Or maybe even life itself."

Sam raised an eyebrow. "Life? As a dimension?"

"Well," Adam said, warming to the idea, "maybe consciousness is the dimension, but life is the force. We always talk about gravity, magnetism, and electromagnetism. But life has a vitality we never put in the same category. Isn't it strange that we can replicate all kinds of forces, but we can only get life from life? Why isn't that its own class of force?"

Sam smirked. "Is this an abortion debate in disguise? Because this is the worst context ever."

Adam laughed. "Dad, no. I'm talking about vitality. The thing that makes sprouts break concrete."

Sam nodded slowly. "Then you may be onto something. Clear as mud—but still intriguing."

Sarah hadn't touched her meal. She was looking at her brother thoughtfully. "Actually," she said, "I've been thinking about your Universe Cake Theory. And I have a way to explain it."

Sam gestured. "We're listening."

Sarah tucked a strand of hair behind her ear and spoke with cautious precision. "You know how sound needs a medium—air or water—for vibrations to travel?"

"Yes," Sam said, leaning forward.

"Well, scientists used to think space was a vacuum—nothingness. Now, most believe the fabric of space is a medium. Light moves through it, like sound through air. So, when they say light can't escape a black hole, maybe it's not because of extreme gravity. Maybe inside a black hole, the medium itself is gone. There's nothing for light to travel through."

Adam placed a hand on his chest in mock injury. "I thought *I* was the mud expert."

Sam chuckled. "Competition's fierce."

For a few seconds, peace settled over the table—a fragile, precious peace. The kind a family finds when, even for a moment, they forget that the world is falling apart.

Sam looked at his children—their restless minds, their bright attempts to understand the universe just as it threatened to collapse on them—and felt pride and grief swell in his chest.

***

Outside, the wind rattled the windows. Far beyond their walls, the first icy fragments streaked across the atmosphere, glowing emerald and cobalt as they dissolved into vapor. From space, the debris glittered like beaded necklaces unraveling across the darkness.

News anchors called them "the fireworks of the end times." Children pointed from rooftops. Skeptics doubled down: pretty lights, nothing more.

But the world was already changing beneath the spectacle.

Sheets of rain became the new rhythm in many parts of the world—not constant, not everywhere, but frequent enough to feel unnatural. In the weeks following the first impacts, most of the fragments fell over open ocean, adding vapor to the atmosphere faster than the planet could shed it. Coastlines swelled. Low-lying districts quietly drowned long before anyone understood the pattern.

In coastal cities, the sea began its slow invasion, creeping inland storm by storm, each tide reaching higher than the last—changes subtle enough that people adapted without realizing how quickly the shoreline was rewriting itself.

In New York, streets filled with salt water during heavy surges until cars floated like forgotten toys. Drones buzzed between skyscrapers, ferrying urgent packages where bridges had become canals. Office towers reflected a new world—Manhattan as a lagoon.

In Mumbai, shantytowns sagged into marsh. Families stacked sandbags in lines that looked like stitched seams on a cloth too fragile to mend.

In Sydney, beloved beaches vanished under a restless tide. Lifeguard towers stood like lonely perches above sweeping gray water.

Inland regions didn't see the ocean, but they heard it: distant impacts, a low continuous rumble, rain that fell cold, steady, and relentless, rivers swelling until fields turned into slick mirrors of mud and standing water.

Yet humanity adapted with stubborn resilience.

In inland areas, classes reopened. Commuters returned to trains. Businesses resumed operations with cautious optimism. People exchanged nervous jokes and shrugged at the sky, trying to pretend the world wasn't changing.

Adam and Sarah, home between semesters, packed for college as if it were any other term, though their movements were slow, distracted. Eisha folded their clothes with methodical care as Sam pretended to check satellite data on his tablet, mostly staring blankly.

The family reviewed their emergency plan—again. A rendezvous point. Backup communication. A promise that if the worst happened, they'd find one another.

When the kids finally left, the car pulled away, a soft spray of rain trailing its tires. Sam and Eisha stood in the doorway long after the taillights vanished, their hands unconsciously tightening around each other's. They didn't speak. They didn't need to. The world was shifting under their feet.

At the university, the illusion of normalcy was beginning to fray. What had once been a faint, ignorable tension during those first uncertain weeks had sharpened into something more urgent. Sirens wailed more often now—no longer simple tests, but real alerts that echoed across the quads. Emergency posters spread across campus like a second skin, taped to doors, stairwells, and lecture hall walls.

Students didn't bother whispering anymore. Conversations broke open in hallways and cafeterias, drifting inevitably toward the same questions: *"How far will this go?"* *"When will it reach us?"* *"Why isn't anyone telling us more?"*

Sam tried to focus on his monitors at home, but something in the air felt off—heavier than before. The distant rumbling had grown louder, deeper, as if the planet itself were bracing.

Then came the night the sky changed.

Above the region, clouds turned a rusty red, lit from within by flashes of eerie green lightning that spiderwebbed across the horizon. The air carried the faint tang of salt, even though the nearest coast was hours away. Static electricity clung to curtains and hair. Birds flew low and frantic, as if trying to hide beneath the earth.

Sam knew the signs. He had been expecting them. But when they finally arrived, he felt a chill that went deeper than bone. The storm had finally come—this time not as rumor, but as reality.

The ocean's mass had grown markedly in just a few days, displacing air and warping weather systems. As more ice fragments vaporized and the atmosphere thickened with moisture, heat bled unevenly across the globe, twisting storms into strange new shapes. Lightning stitched the sky into a luminous web. From orbit, Earth still looked peaceful—soft, blue, luminous—but beneath that beauty hid a churning imbalance.

Sam's region had been spared the worst so far. But every model he ran said the same thing: the reprieve wouldn't last.

Those who lived on high ground had counted themselves lucky, watching the chaos unfold from a distance. But distance was an illusion, and luck was running out.

It began with the thuds. A crack. A rumble. A blast of air that shook tiles loose from roofs. Icy grains fell like glittering hail, collecting in gutters and on lawns. Windows cracked in spiderweb patterns. Trees bent under sudden gusts of frigid wind.

Sam watched from his window, brow furrowed. "These are just the appetizers."

Color drained from Eisha's face. "Appetizers?"

Sam nodded grimly. "The models show a denser cluster approaching. Hours away, maybe less."

He reached for his communicator and dialed the kids. It rang once. Twice. The connection flickered.

No answer.

"Try again," Eisha whispered.

He did. Still nothing.

A silence more profound than any storm settled over them. It felt like the beginning of a war.

The main event struck not with thunder, but with light. A blinding flash—blue, then white—saturated their windows, even through the curtains. The house quaked. The power went out so abruptly that the darkness felt like a blow.

Seconds later, a shock wave tore through the walls. Air pressure slammed into them. Dust rained from the ceiling. Glass shattered somewhere inside the house.

"Back of the house!" Sam shouted.

They grabbed flashlights, stumbling through hallways that seemed to sway under their feet. The air was thick with a metallic smell—heated iron and ozone.

When Sam yanked open the back door, the canal that once glowed quietly beneath moonlight had become a roiling mass of water. Their floater dock—Harbor 7—was already half-submerged, its lights flickering like a dying heartbeat. Mooring lines strained, then snapped one by one with sharp, violent cracks.

"Oh my God…" Eisha gasped. "It's not gradual. It's … it's here!"

In the distance, a communications tower collapsed in a cascade of sparks and twisted metal. Sirens wailed throughout the city, long, mournful, almost human.

Sam sprinted toward the emergency boat. Water surged to his knees as he forced his way forward. "Eisha, grab the pack!"

She turned to run back inside—

—and the house split apart.

A deep crack tore down the wall with the sound of splitting stone. A surge of water burst through, sweeping furniture, dishes, shards of glass, and insulation with it. The kitchen table spun like a leaf caught in a current. Eisha screamed as the wave knocked her off her feet. Sam lunged, caught her arm, and dragged her upright, both of them gasping as icy water swirled around their waists.

They fought through the chaos toward the boat as another surge lifted it clear off the dock. Sam hauled himself in and reached for Eisha just as the last mooring lines snapped.

The boat lurched. The world tilted. And the house—*their* house—was torn apart behind them, swallowed into the rising sea.

"Sam!" Eisha cried, clinging to the railing. "The kids—"

Static hissed from the radio. Voices flickered:

"*... structural collapse ...*"

"*... power grid down ...*"

"*... multiple impact zones ...*"

"*... university ...*"

The last word hit Sam like an impact of its own. He grabbed the radio, hands shaking. "This is Dr. Sam Saphire—my children are at the university. Do you read?"

The signal flickered. Crackled. Died.

Sam slammed the console. "Come on!"

Nothing.

"When this wave slows," he said, forcing calm into his voice, "we'll go for them."

"But—"

"No what-ifs."

Eisha clung to his arm, trembling.

Then the second wave came.

What fell from the sky was no gentle shower of icicles. This was artillery from the heavens. Massive chunks—some the size of stadiums, others like small mountains—tumbled through the atmosphere like rogue moons. Some scraped the upper air and skipped off, leaving trails of glowing vapor. Others plunged straight down, smothering everything in their path.

44

A shard the size of a skyscraper slammed into the North Atlantic. Satellites captured the plume rising hundreds of miles. Hours later, a monstrous wave struck Ireland and Britain. Entire towns vanished under walls of water higher than cathedrals.

Another impact hit the Pacific, raising a column of spray so tall that it cast a shadow for miles. Island chains disappeared; entire fleets vanished.

Everywhere, after each strike, came the hail—thin icy fragments pulverized from larger masses. They fell like glittering dust at first, then like glassy snow, layering rooftops and melting into frigid runoff.

Sam gripped the controls harder with each distant blast, his knuckles white.

Still, the water rose. Not all at once—but hour by hour, surge by surge. New York drowned deeper. Rivers in Europe reversed course. Monsoon basins spilled over Asia. Russia's far north cracked under the weight of falling ice.

And beyond the chaotic headlines flashing across the emergency bands, the quiet truth settled in: this was only the beginning.

***

As days passed, Sam's region became unrecognizable. The familiar grid of streets had transformed into a fractured sea. Houses floated half-submerged. Vehicles bobbed in churning currents. Lampposts leaned like reeds in a storm. Their boat drifted over places that had once defined their lives—over the grocery store where Sarah used to stop after school, over the park where Adam had learned to ride a bike, over the café where Sam and Eisha had their first date. Everything was gone.

They passed survivors clinging to a billboard ripped from its supports. One man waved desperately, shouting, but the currents were too strong. Sam threw a line that fell heartbreakingly short.

"Hold on!" he shouted. "Find something higher! Keep climbing!"

But higher ground was disappearing.

A deceptive stillness settled. The surface calmed. The fragments overhead thinned. Sam dared to hope...

Then the tremor came.

A deep vibration rolled beneath their boat like a giant awakening. A dark line sharpened on the horizon—another surge, taller and faster than any before.

Eisha gripped his sleeve. "Tell me that's not—"

"It is."

The ocean rose like a creature standing upright.

"You said it wouldn't be devastating!" Eisha cried, her voice cracking.

"I was wrong,"

The words were heavier than the wave itself.

The surge struck.

Water swallowed the boat, lifting and dropping it violently. The world became roaring wind, splintering wood, stinging spray.

Eisha screamed, clinging to Sam as the boat twisted sideways. Lightning flashed, thunder bellowed, and the boat was like a toy caught in a whirlpool.

And then...

Darkness.

The darkness gave way to days that blurred into one another. Then nights. Then something in between.

The world became water.

Storms raged. Rain fell in relentless sheets, turning the sky into a single, trembling curtain. Ice shards hissed as they melted on contact with the sea. Winds howled with a voice so deep, it drowned out human cries.

Sam and Eisha's boat was tossed endlessly across an apocalyptic ocean. Sometimes they went for hours without speaking. Sometimes they whispered their children's names like a prayer. Sleep came in fragments, stolen between jolts of thunder and the slamming of waves.

When transmissions broke through the static, they came as ghosts of messages:

"... *East Atlantic sector ... gone...* "

"... *no contact with the Mars colony ...* "

"... *rescue efforts suspended ...* "

"... *sea level rising faster than ...* "

Each message tightened the cold knot in Sam's chest.

One night, the radio crackled weakly:

"... *university district ...* "

"… cannot hold…"

"… communications failing…"

Eisha's sob cut straight through the storm. Sam pulled her close, offering reassurances he barely believed.

Days stretched into more days. The water kept rising—not in violent leaps now, but in a steady, merciless climb. The constant rain, the melting hail, and the global deluge from surviving fragments all fed a planet drowning inch by inch, hour by hour.

***

Weeks later, the storms softened. Not cleared—never cleared—but softened, as if exhaustion had reached even the sky.

The light dimmed to an eerie amber. The rain eased into a ghostly mist. Debris drifted past in slow procession—solar panels, a toy car, the railing of someone's porch.

Eisha hugged her knees, her eyes following each piece. "What if they're looking for us too? What if they're out there somewhere, waiting … hoping we're alive?"

Sam reached into the waterproof kit and pulled out the compass. The needle spun wildly at first, confused by magnetic distortion. Then, finally, it steadied.

North.

"We head for the ridges," he said softly. "If anything's left standing, it'll be there."

Eisha nodded. "The kids… They'd think the same." A small, trembling smile. "And they'd mock your navigation."

For the first time in weeks, she laughed.

***

Nights remained cold. Sometimes Eisha woke up claiming someone had called her name. She would grip Sam's arm, gasping, then curl inward, grieving quietly in the dark. Sam stayed beside her, whispering comfort he wasn't sure he could provide.

During the days, they skirted rooftops jutting above the water like jagged rocks. Sam scanned the horizon for land or survivors. Sometimes he spotted a distant silhouette waving from a drifting structure, but the currents carried them apart before they could get close.

The world had become a graveyard of memories. And yet, Sam refused to surrender hope.

They drifted over what had once been their city. He could almost trace the ghostly lines beneath the water—faint, parallel markings that had once been Adam and Sarah's bike route.

The silence thickened around them.

Then—a cry. A thin, distant cry sliced the stillness.

Sam stiffened. Eisha bolted upright.

Above them, a gull circled, white wings carving through the amber sky. Its call echoed bright and clear, impossibly alive. It wheeled once, glided northward, and disappeared into the mist.

Sam watched it go. A single gull. Proof of life. Proof that the world was still capable of enduring—of offering signs, even in ruin.

Ocean Earth

The storm ended not with silence, but with exhaustion—like a giant drawing its final breath after weeks of tearing the world apart. For days on end, rain had screamed against the planet, hammering roofs until they dissolved and forests until they bowed. Now the Earth seemed emptied, spent, incapable of producing even one more drop. Clouds sagged low and bruised across the sky, torn in places where thin, trembling fingers of sunlight slipped through. Below them, an unbroken sheet of water stretched to every horizon, swallowing the last memory of where land had been. It looked like a world reset—washed clean and hollowed out.

Those who survived awoke slowly, dazed beneath the strange new light. They drifted in small boats or clung to rafts, refrigerator doors, shattered planks—anything that floated. There was no orientation now—no north, no city grid, no shoreline to anchor the mind. Only water, and the ruins of what once gave humanity its shape.

A refrigerator bobbed next to a roof tile. A child's swing tangled itself in torn cables and floating debris. A dog paddled in exhausted circles until a survivor lifted it from the waves.

But the eerie calm on the surface revealed nothing of the devastation beneath. Bodies drifted beside overturned cars and fragments of kitchens. Birds circled low, landing briefly on anything solid before leaping skyward again. From time to time, an engine coughed somewhere—a survivor coaxing life from a half-drowned motor—before fading into the hiss of wind moving across the newborn ocean.

Voices began calling across the emptiness—desperate, lonely, or hopeful. Sometimes one answered back. Sometimes it didn't. People clung to barrels, tables, roof beams, instinctively drifting toward one another. Fear separated them; survival stitched them together.

Within days, clusters formed: boats tied together with frayed ropes, rafts lashed edge to edge, tiny islands of humanity rising from the flood.

Sam Saphire sat half awake in the modest vessel that had carried him and Eisha through the worst of the chaos. Though the waves had gentled, each crest brought debris from their past life—splintered signs, broken furniture, things that had no business in the sea.

Across from him, Eisha stared silently at the horizon, her eyes unfocused, her expression caught between disbelief and grief.

After a long, trembling silence, she whispered, "Everything is gone."

Sam didn't trust himself to speak. He only nodded. His throat felt raw. Every landmark, every familiar street, every place tied to memory—vanished beneath the water. Civilization had been peeled from the Earth like the skin of a fruit, leaving only the swelling ocean beneath.

They spent hours scanning the emptiness with salt-streaked binoculars. At last, something emerged—a tall, straight line in the distance. A high-rise. Its upper floors jutted from the flood, glass panels glinting weakly in the pale morning light.

"Downtown," Sam murmured. "That's what's left of it."

Around the building, debris had formed a halo—boats, containers, roof fragments. People were climbing, gesturing, calling. The drowned city center had become a fragile sanctuary.

Eisha's breath caught. "Maybe they're there. Maybe Adam and Sarah climbed up—found someone—made it to the higher floors—"

Sam lowered the binoculars. "We'll check. We will."

They angled their craft toward the cluster, rowing more often than motoring. Fuel had become sacred; their generator sat half-submerged, groaning with every swell.

The water became a drifting museum of memories. A church roof floated past, its steeple snapped clean off. A sign rolled lazily in a swell—*Welcome to Riverside Mall*, the letters warped into a cruel joke.

Suddenly, a thin cry carried across the water.

Two men clung to a warped beam, knuckles white. Sam maneuvered close and dragged them aboard. One stared upward, unblinking; the other shivered uncontrollably, mumbling fragments of lost thoughts. A shoe floated nearby—whose, no one could tell. Hard to know. Harder to ask. Survival was the only currency now.

By dusk, improvised systems began to take shape.

Those with radios powered them by hand crank or with small solar panels. When night fell, scattered lanterns and phones—glowing weakly from whatever charge remained, not for communication but simply as light—flickered across the horizon—hundreds of tiny lights swaying on the water like new constellations.

Eisha watched them, transfixed. "They're signaling."

"Yeah," Sam murmured. "Communities are forming."

Small lights blinked across the newly made ocean as if the night sky had fallen into the water—humanity's new atlas, points of fragile hope drifting in a darkened world.

Morse code ticked softly across the waves. Radios crackled with weary voices trading coordinates and rumors of surviving landmarks. And always, behind the noise, came the distant thunder of impacts—sporadic now, weaker, but still terrifying.

Survivors around the half-sunken high-rise began lashing vessels together to create a buoyant perimeter. Supplies were pooled, platforms shared. Someone painted a name on a sheet of plywood: NORTH HARBOR ONE.

A man with a salvaged receiver relayed what news he could gather.

"… Europe mostly underwater… Highland pockets intact… Asia's mountain chains above sea level… Faint signals… Mars transmitting every few days…"

"Coordination?" Sam asked. "With who?"

"Anyone alive."

He tapped the cracked earphones against his head, adjusting them gently. "Mars is coming through clearly—actual voice transmissions, not just static.. Governor Jay Peters himself."

Sam leaned closer. "What are they saying?"

"That they were hit, but nothing like we were. Thousands of impacts. Dust storms for weeks." He lifted a soggy notebook. "Earth took the hammer. Mars caught the handle."

The man hesitated. "They mentioned you, Dr. Saphire. Governor Peters said your warning bought them precious weeks. Called you 'the voice that saved Mars.'"

The words struck Sam harder than any wave.

Eisha gripped his hand. "They heard you."

"And they say they'll come back. Not now—years. But they repeat it every message: 'Hold the line. We will return.'"

For the first time since the rain began, the horizon looked like a doorway instead of a grave.

Scavenging soon became more than a necessity; it became a ritual, a choreography of hope and desperation. The ocean offered odd treasures: barrels of oil, plastic crates, soaked mattresses, broken doors. Suitcases drifted open like gutted fish, spilling out shirts, books, fragments of people's former lives. Survivors paddled through debris fields as if browsing the aisles in a macabre supermarket. A wooden door became a raft. A cabinet became a platform. A plastic bin became a pantry. Nothing was useless, not even the broken things.

But nothing prepared them for the animals.

It began with a pair of deer drifting on a fallen tree limb, hooves slipping on the smooth bark. Then came a horse, massive and trembling—swimming in panicked circles, until a cluster of boats formed a ring around it and guided it to a platform. People wrapped it in blankets, whispering reassurances none of them fully believed.

Birds soon became the sky's currency. Seagulls nested on masts. Pelicans followed fishing boats like silent escorts. Songbirds fluttered onto open palms, too weak to fear anything.

Nature, too, was improvising—reshaping itself to fit the new world.

Each evening, the survivors quieted. The first days' adrenaline, sharp as lightning, faded into a deeper, trembling fatigue. The sky darkened. Radio static hummed. Lanterns and battery lamps blinked to life, floating pinpricks marking the fragile beginnings of civilization. People cried suddenly—the kind of tears that come only after you've survived the unthinkable.

Across the world, millions stirred from half-sleep—in boats, on rafts, in half-broken ships, in the rib cages of fallen buildings, in fragments of the old world that refused to sink.

The rain had stopped. Thunder had retreated into memory. What remained was quieter—a vast hush broken only by waves brushing against the remnants of civilization.

***

That evening, Eisha sat beside Sam at the edge of their platform, staring into the black mirror of the water. "I keep seeing faces," she murmured. "In the reflections. I know they're not real ... but I keep seeing them."

Sam didn't answer immediately. Sunset bled across the horizon, staining the water a muted orange. The skyline's remains looked like a broken promise.

"That's where they'll come," Sam said softly. "The kids. They'll see the lights. They'll head this way."

"If the current brings them," she whispered.

"If the current brings them," he echoed.

The sea rocked them gently—comfort without safety.

Sam's thoughts drifted to seasons—spring blooms, autumn leaves, the smell of soil. All gone. No flowers left to blossom, no trees to lose their leaves. Would Earth now have only one endless season of water?

He imagined creatures evolving—amphibious survivors shaped by necessity. Then he pictured bees—the tiny stewards of life. Would they endure? How could they? He imagined one lone bee drifting across the boundless sea, searching for a flower that no longer existed.

Maybe some things survived only as memory—and maybe memory itself was how the Earth kept living.

Cities no longer existed in any meaningful way. Mountains were islands now—peaks rising from the flood. Highways curled beneath the water like lost rivers. Nations had become coordinates carried through static. Old maps were relics, depicting a land that no longer existed.

The ships that survived became humanity's new continents: cargo giants, cruise liners, aircraft carriers—each transformed into a floating city whose captain suddenly bore the weight of an entire civilization. Some ships became democratic, others authoritarian. Some drifted, ruled by whoever had fuel. Some wandered alone, ghost vessels of the new age.

Between them floated tethered communities—flotillas bound together by rope, shared food, and fragile hope.

It was among one such cluster that Sam and Eisha found Haven-3.

Haven-3 had begun as an engineering project built quietly by Rafi—broad-shouldered, stubborn, practical in a way the old world had never appreciated. Before the impacts, he had designed a modular flotilla: metal platforms, shipping containers, walkways, emergency solar fields, deepwater anchors designed to hold even with the rising sea. When the waters surged, Haven-3 didn't drown; it lifted.

By the time Sam and Eisha reached it, more than two thousand survivors had gathered—floating hospitals fashioned from cruise-ship tops, food storage inside cargo containers, tents pitched across the steel decks of old warships. Solar panels shimmered like metallic lily pads. Desalination tanks hissed softly. Smoke curled from makeshift kitchens. The city swayed and creaked, but it held.

Sam stepped aboard like a man stepping into purpose. His scientific instincts—analysis, troubleshooting, stabilizing chaos—

became survival tools. He worked immediately: repairing solar arrays, recalibrating desalination units, reprogramming salvaged radios.

"Food first," Rafi told him.

"Communication is food," Sam replied.

They locked eyes, then nodded. They were both right.

Life fell into a steady rhythm, equal parts cooperation and exhaustion. Morning: ration lines and fishing patrols. Midday: repairs, patching hulls, tending nets. Evening: communal meals. Night: hope.

And the animals, miraculously, became a part of it. Some livestock had been airlifted in desperate final hours: goats, chickens, a dozen cows. They were not merely animals now; they were infrastructure. Milk and eggs became currency. Dogs wandered the decks. Cats slipped between containers. Deer appeared on platforms until survivors rescued them and guided them to improvised floating sanctuaries. Birds nested everywhere—seagulls in the rigging, hawks on antennas, pelicans circling like sentinels. Their presence comforted people. If birds had survived, perhaps humanity could, too.

Survival blurred the line between wild and tame.

Meals became rituals. Survivors gathered around metal drums packed with driftwood or broken furniture, listening to flames crackle against steel. Fires reflected on the water like tiny suns. People shared stories—not always of the storm, but of life before it. How they'd escaped. Who they'd lost. What they remembered of land. Names were spoken like prayers. Shared grief became warmth. Memories became communal property. It was how the dead remained alive.

Food became an expression of gratitude. A single ripe orange passed from hand to hand symbolized hope. Hydroponic trays salvaged from rooftop gardens or greenhouses began to yield small harvests—lettuce, herbs, even tomatoes. Every sprout was celebrated.

The old world's excess became unthinkable. People joked about supermarkets now—aisles of soap, endless cereal choices, shelves of snacks. Now, a bar of soap was precious. A toothbrush was gold.

Though an ocean of water surrounded them, none of it was safe to drink. Desalination units ran constantly, hissing like tired beasts. Each person received a strict daily ration. Bathing was a weekly blessing—ten minutes under a lukewarm solar bag.

At night, the water glowed. Mineral-rich meltwater from the ice triggered vast blooms of bioluminescent plankton. Waves shimmered with electric blue. Entire flotillas drifted through corridors of living light—eerie, beautiful, comforting. It was proof that life had not died—only transformed.

But for Sam and Eisha, everything narrowed down to a single purpose: finding Adam and Sarah.

Every time the satellite array blinked awake, Sam sent the same message:

"This is Dr. Sam Saphire of Haven-3. Grid 24.872 N, 63.204 W. Searching for Adam and Sarah Saphire. Please confirm."

Only static came in response—until one night, a faint robotic voice murmured: *"Message received. Data logged."*

Sam clung to that scrap of hope.

***

A month later, the evening air carried a rare calm when a soft chime echoed across Haven-3. Radios crackled. Lights flickered. People froze.

Then, a transmission:

"Attention, surviving communities: this is Central Earth Coordination—Mars Colony Relay One…"

Haven-3 erupted. Strangers hugged. Others fell to their knees. Rafi shouted for the council, voice shaking.

"They're listening!"

Sam's breath trembled. "We're not alone."

Through the night, Sam and the engineers strengthened the signal—rigging old antennas, salvaging copper coils, powering systems with solar-charged capacitors. Every successful ping sent joy through the flotilla.

Then, for the first time, a complete message arrived:

"This is President Landers."

Silence swept over the flotilla.

"To all who can hear me—on every ship, in every settlement— know this: we are still here. Cities have fallen. Countless lives have been lost. But many have survived. We will rebuild. This world is

changed—but it is still ours. Stay alive. Stay connected. And when you can … answer back."

When the broadcast ended, the silence felt sacred.

Sam whispered, "He made it."

"And so did we," Eisha murmured.

***

In the weeks that followed, flotillas that once drifted quietly now hummed with overlapping signals. Smaller communities like Haven-3 reported to newly formed megacenters—Atlantica, New Geneva, Pacifica, clusters of ships welded into floating capitals.

Relay buoys were dropped into the sea like seeds, each one bouncing messages to satellites that had somehow survived. Ancient servers sealed in mountain vaults came online again, their backups forming the digital skeleton of a civilization washed away.

At dawn and dusk, the airwaves buzzed:

"Sector Nine reporting—thirty-eight survivors, two infants."

"Haven Twelve, requesting medical support."

"Drift pods from East Africa sighted—repeat, East Africa confirmed."

"Pacifica requesting desalination filters."

Every message was a heartbeat, every reply a pulse. Earth—wounded, flooded, transformed—was breathing again.

Still, survival remained fragile. Fuel dwindled. Solar panels corroded in the salty air. Waste collected in swirling gyres that glimmered beneath the waves.

Haven-3 adopted strict rules: Organic waste to sea. Metal and plastic to sorting. Cloth and fiber to insulation and rope. Nothing wasted. Nothing forgotten.

At first, these rules seemed desperate. But something unexpected happened: the ocean responded.

Organic matter fed plankton blooms. Fish schools multiplied. Corals began glowing faintly on submerged ruins, pale halos clinging to what had once been streets and homes.

Sam often leaned over the railing, watching the teeming life below.

"We give back what we take," he told Eisha, "and the sea remembers kindness."

It became a saying—half joke, half prayer.

The sea became sustenance, memory, and mirror. Nets returned not only with fish, but with fragments of the past: Waterlogged books. Toys still smiling. Clothing sealed tight in plastic. What had once been pollution had become providence. What had once been junk had become infrastructure.

Drifting laboratories—converted barges manned by scientists, medics, and salvaged AI—mapped debris cycles, tracking how currents transformed destruction into a new supply chain. Each item carried a story. A wooden playground railing from a town a thousand miles away. A tablet with a family photo burned permanently into its lifeless screen—a family photo. A window frame from a home Sam and Eisha once passed on weekend walks. People no longer called these things trash. They were the keepsakes of a drowned world.

In shallower regions, where the land had not sunk too deeply or the water had risen unevenly, something extraordinary remained. Entire neighborhoods preserved beneath clear blue water—streets, schoolyards, park benches. Roofs dusted with coral. Stoplights pointing nowhere. Cars still perfectly parked, as if waiting for owners who would never return.

Families went diving with scuba gear or just simple goggles. Others free-dived, drifting above their old lives. They traced invisible roads with their hands. Pressed palms to submerged windows. Hovered over their old porches and closed their eyes. Some retrieved small treasures—framed photos, jewelry boxes, journals. Salvage teams often paused when someone surfaced crying, clutching a fragile memory.

"You can feel the silence down there," one survivor said quietly. "Like the world is holding its breath."

Some said the underwater towns were more beautiful than they ever were in life. Others could not bear to look at all.

Communities developed cultures of their own—structured city-nations with councils. Flotilla schools taught math through buoyancy—using barrels, rafts, and water displacement as the new chalk and slate. Nomadic rafts trading fish for tools, wanderers who preferred the solitude of the open sea. Ghost ships drifting silently through the fog became the new folklore—stories whispered between flotillas.

Animals adapted, too—ducks weaving through barges, cats exploring decks, dogs balancing easily on rafts, dolphins guiding stragglers back toward larger groups. Nature was stitching itself back together through the world that remained.

Haven-3, like every floating city, was organized chaos—but it was alive. People laughed. Argued. Helped one another. Shared food. Shared stories. Shared grief. Sang at night when the waves were kind. Dreamed in fragments.

Humanity had not vanished. It had changed—fundamentally, and in many ways, beautifully. And in that change, it rediscovered something long forgotten: How to live with little. How to share. How to hope. How to survive without excess. How to recognize the miracle of a single orange, a working radio, a living child. The world had drowned, yes. But in the drowning, something new had risen—a quieter, humbler version of humankind, still clinging to life, still searching for one another across the endless blue.

The Search for the Lost

Sam never stopped counting battery minutes. He kept the little field radio wrapped in foam and oilskin, the way sailors once cradled flares—an object not of convenience, but of survival. Every dawn and dusk, he keyed in the same beacon pattern: three short beeps, two long, one short. Then he powered down. They could trickle-charge from the solar drape —the small roll-out survival kit panel—if the sky cooperated, but every watt had to serve more than hope.

"Smart, not random," Eisha reminded him each morning.

"Signals help only if our radios are powered—and we're alive to hear the reply."

Across the water world, survivors stitched themselves into something that resembled society. Big ships became floating utilities and rationing councils. Small towns like Haven-3 learned to stretch their limitations into strengths. Out of necessity, a vast drifting registry formed, each settlement keeping a ledger of the missing and the found. Once a week, packets of names pulsed across "the mesh," a living database any mayor could copy, update, and circulate.

Sam and Eisha visited the registry kiosk every morning after receiving their rations. They learned the choreography of searching for your own: flip laminated sheets, scan columns of names and last-known coordinates, hold your breath while scanning through the alphabet. Hope snagged on near-matches like false promises, then bled away quietly.

"Not today," Eisha would say, steady for others, trembling only for herself.

"Tomorrow," Sam would answer.

Some nights, a cry of joy rippled across the decks as someone calling out faint but familiar names through the static. Strangers gathered instinctively, cheering for one anothers' reunions. But for every shout, there were a hundred silent heartbreaks—people tapping their own radios, recalibrating dials in sudden superstition, whispering prayers into plastic and wires. The same unspoken question carried them all to sleep: what if that call never came?

Eisha found rhythm in the ache. Two-hour kitchen shifts meant one proper meal a day for anyone who could stand in line; everything else was simple and spare. The handyman crew—half the town, really—drifted from repaired hinge to hinge, patching civilization with rope, stainless steel screws, and patience. Orphaned children belonged to everyone until a name in the registry stitched them back to family. Hydroponic tubes sprouted beans and spinach along the rails. Schools reappeared under tarps: math and language, yes, but also how simple circuits were repaired, how pumps were dismantled and rebuilt. The future, after all, might need to start over from scratch.

A month passed. Then another. The registry grew thick with the found. The government communication windows stabilized just enough for mayors to trade weather guesses and convoy routes through the few satellites that still functioned. Floating towns traded copper, desalinated water, and news the way the old world had traded stock tips.

Sam's hope thinned to a wire—but held. Sleep had abandoned him, so he took the graveyard watch at the registry station. With a headlamp and a fresh packet from a megacenter, he read slowly, unwilling to trust the janky text-scanner someone had built from an old phone and a salvaged lens. He was three pages deep when he almost missed it: Alan Surefire—misfiled under *T*—tagged to a rope city called Trellis Sound. Last contact: voice beacon received, battery weak, seeking convoy passage.

"Alan Surefire… *Adam Saphire?*" Sam murmured. In a world where static obscured half of every syllable, certainty was a luxury.

He typed in the family keyword—*Bluebell*—and waited with the patience of a man holding his breath beneath ice. Nothing. He tried again.

A teenage clerk with a sailor's knot tattoo touched his shoulder gently.

"Mesh is patchy at this hour," the boy said. "Try again at dawn."

Eisha leaned over, watching the thin green waveform crawl across the screen. "You think it could be Adam?"

"After all," Sam breathed, throat tight, "who would really be named Surefire?"

Doubt collapsed into determination.

"If there's even a one-in-a-thousand chance," he said, "I have to go."

"Not just to look," Eisha said softly. "To find them."

***

By morning, the east wore a lion's mane of cloud. Mayor Rafi lit the council lanterns early and called in logistics.

"You've done your part here," he told them. "Here will keep. Go."

They readied Haven-3's search skiff with almost ritual care: dual engines—solar-electric by day, small gas backup for night or storms—plus spare battery packs nestled like sleeping animals, jerry cans lashed under benches, flares, lines, med kit, and a hand-inked chart of ropeways, annotated with old sailors' superstitions. Mira, the sharp-eared comms tech, and Tareek, the pilot with cable-thick fingers, volunteered to crew. Rafi gave them what every leader gives when nothing else remains: permission they didn't need, and a blessing they did.

They moved by day, the engine humming, the skiff sliding along ropeways like a bead on a taut line. At each friendly rig, they bartered copper for diesel and left breadcrumbs: SAPHIRE — H3 — BLUEBELL — DAWNLINE — SEEKING ADAM/SARAH — HEADING EAST — CONTACT ANY RELAY.

***

Port Willow rose from the swells like a quilt built from need—barges welded to decks, bottle-lanterns trembling in the breeze. A salt-and-pepper-haired man waved them in.

"Marco," he greeted them. "Harbormaster by trade, mayor by default. Everyone still comes to me when they need something trimmed … or lifted."

He showed them around the makeshift store, where nets dried on the rails and barefoot children darted between the crates.

That night, the townsfolk brought fish, boiled roots, and jars of collected rainwater to share around a dock fire. Grief bent into laughter in that circle—a man riding in a floating bathtub who called himself Iceberg Pete; a woman who bragged she had once hooked a fish with the underwire of her bra. For a few minutes, the sea sounded like a neighborhood again.

"Keep an eye on your gear," Marco warned before they turned in for the night.

Just before dawn, Eisha woke to a hush that wasn't the sea or wind. Something in the air felt wrong. She sat up sharply.

The crate was gone. Her cry split the morning.

Sam tore back tarps and overturned benches. When the truth set in, his knees failed him. The radios weren't just equipment; they were lifelines—the only real bridge to Adam and Sarah.

Word raced through Port Willow like an oil fire. In this new world, you did not steal a man's radio. It was his horse in the Wild West, his map, his legs, his hope. Lanterns swung wildly as searchers combed catwalks, children peered into barrels, and women cradled their own radios like infants.

Dusk found Sam sitting on the dock, staring at the dark water in silence.

"If they call tonight," breathed, "and I can't answer…"

71

Just before full dark, two foster parents arrived with two shivering teens and the oil-wrapped radios.

"We didn't realize," the boy sobbed. "We didn't think—"

"You didn't just take devices," Sam said, voice scraped raw. "You took hope."

"They understand," the foster father murmured.

"Thank you," Eisha said, her hands trembling as she took the radios back.

The kids nodded, terrified and remorseful.

Later, as they sat guard beside the crate, Eisha whispered, "Feels like the universe has it in for us."

"Then we make it listen," Sam said.

They pushed on.

***

Dock Nine brought an unexpected reunion. The barber who'd cut Sam's hair since grad school sobbed into his apron and laid out polished scissors like relics. "Your children?" he asked.

"No news," Eisha said.

He nodded as if acknowledging a difficult diagnosis. Keep moving forward.

Boyle's Yard, a café built in a shipping container, buzzed with barter. The owner remembered their kids fixing his fridge and doing homework in a corner booth.

"They're not here," he said, chalking SAPHIRE — SEEKING onto a slate already thick with names. "But if they come through, I'll tell them you were here—and that you're searching for them."

Storms didn't wait for forecasts. A blue squall soon unzipped the horizon and swallowed the world. Tareek dropped a sea anchor, and they rode it out. The weather was an erratic temper now, not a predictable system. When the curtain lifted, everything smelled of ozone and washed metal. Even under bad light, the solar drapes had gulped enough sun. The radio lived.

At night, they drifted. Phytoplankton wrote cursive in light in their wake. Strangers padded down the planks offering soup, stories, or simply company. Clear nights were thick with stars; rain turned the deck into a drum. Through these encounters, Sam learned the new arithmetic of survival—not ownership, but shared warmth.

Rope Crown appeared as lanterns came on for the night. Painted in bold letters across a gate: SHARE TO PASS.

Eisha paid with medicine and news—real currency. The harbormaster nodded approvingly and poured kelp sweet tea.

"Four came through," the woman told them. "Two older, two younger. No names. But the young man counted in patterns." She tapped her thigh: *one-two-three, one-two-three-four, pause.*

Sam's heart skipped. It was Adam's old rhythm for taming panic.

"They were eastbound," she added. "Convoy toward Trellis Sound."

They left at first light. The air itself hummed oddly, lifting the hair on Sam's arms. The radio squealed at a frequency only birds could appreciate. Mira lifted the antenna degree by degree until the squeal fractured into language.

Three short. Two long. One short.

Sam answered immediately. The return signal dopplered—far, near, far again, bouncing along some broken internal coast.

Mira switched to the registry sideband. Compressed text packets crawled in—names, codes, timestamps like barnacle scars. The header flagged *Trellis Sound & Adjuncts*. Sam hunched over the screen, scrolling until the letters blurred.

There it was—cleaner now, filed correctly.

ADAM SAPHIRE — STATUS: Located (awaiting convoy)

SARAH SAPHIRE — STATUS: Located with ADAM

Device compromised; GPS functional; escort arranged.

Sam sent "Bluebell" and "Dawnline" until the radio chewed up his words and spat back static.

Eisha laid a steady hand over his. "They're in motion," she said. "Moving people miss windows. We won't."

They raced toward Trellis Sound, then toward Lattice 5, then toward the rendezvous stamped into their search packet like a promise. At every rig they crossed, someone had a piece of the story—rumors about two teenagers who might have been their children: a girl with a soda-tab bracelet; a boy who counted pump rhythms to predict failure; two students hauling a drowned radio belonging to a third roommate. None of it proved anything. And yet, all of it did.

On their second night out, Haven-3 flagged their hull ID on the mesh.

URGENT: *Mayor requests contact at dawn.*

Rafi did not use "urgent" without cause.

Sam barely slept. He counted phantom beeps in the dark and rehearsed grief he refused to accept.

***

Dawn came suddenly, like a door opening.

The radio crackled. "Incoming message," Mira said sharply.

"*Haven-3 to Search Skiff One.*"

"Skiff One," Sam replied. The words tasted like *"I'm here."*

"*Stand by for patch,*" Rafi's voice said gently. "*Someone wants to speak with you.*"

Silence stretched—then broke.

"*Hey, Dad.*"

"*Hi, Dad,*" another voice said—and that second "Dad" made Eisha clutch her mouth as if the world might spill out of her.

"Adam? Sarah?" Sam's voice cracked like old wood.

"*We're okay,*" Adam said—older by months, older by a lifetime. "*We traveled with a Trellis convoy. Our radio drowned when the storm hit our town, but the GPS survived. At first, nothing was organized.*"

75

We kept missing communication windows—and when we finally got a message out on borrowed radios, we never knew if you could hear."

"We heard enough," Eisha said, her laugh a sob as she tried to remember how to smile. "Where are you now?"

"Haven-3," Sarah said quickly, words tripping over one another. *"At Mayor Rafi's workstation. We met people you'd love. They taught us to fillet fish, and how not to electrocute ourselves while charging batteries. One teacher turned a laundry tent into a school. We fixed three pumps with coat hangers and a prayer."*

"Of course you did," Eisha whispered, crying freely now. "Of course."

"We're east of Rope Crown," Sam said. "Wait for us."

"Travel safe," Adam replied. *"People know your name, Dad. You helped builda mesh that actually works."*

"It works because you're in it," Sam said, and only realized the truth of his words as they left his mouth.

"Ten minutes until the window closes," Rafi warned gently. *"Say what matters."*

What mattered rushed out in helpless, overlapping fragments—"Are you eating? ... Warm? ... Safe? ... Do your fingers still go numb when you're anxious? ... Have you kept the scar on your knee clean? ... Are you scared? ... Are you with good people?"

"Yes... Yes... Kinda... No... Yes... Yes... Sometimes."

"Stay right where you are," Eisha breathed. "We're coming for you."

"You always were," Adam said softly.

The communications window snapped shut like a book.

***

At last, they returned to Haven-3 that afternoon under a sky that finally remembered how to be kind. The convoy eased in with practiced grace, black sails furled, decks tidy, faces along the rails—some young, some lined, all hungry with hope.

And then, they appeared.

Adam, leaner and taller, hair sun-bleached and wild. Sarah, steady on her feet, her soda-tab bracelet glinting like silver. Eisha made the sound she had made the day they were born and was already running, and then everyone was running, and suddenly the decks were too small to hold the size of that moment.

Sam and Eisha laughed and cried and scolded and counted fingers, as if the flood might have stolen some without permission. The convoy crew looked away with the polite instinct of people who lived inches apart and still understood privacy. Mira wiped her eyes discreetly. Tareek handed Adam a coil of line, and Adam took it automatically, muscle memory bridging his past life to the new one.

That night, Haven-3 became a constellation. Lanterns ringed the council deck; a salvaged guitar rediscovered chords; hydroponics techs had produced a single orange and passed it hand to hand like a sacred relic. Rafi keyed the mic with ceremony.

"Haven-3 to Relay," he said. "Reporting two survivors reunited: Adam and Sarah Saphire. Critical needs unchanged. Morale ... improved beyond measure."

"Copy, Haven-3," came the reply—faint, steady, impossibly calm.

The sea breathed. Haven-3 breathed with it. And for the first time since the waters rose, Sam placed the radios back in their oilskin cradle without counting the minutes left on the battery.

***

The next night, after most of Haven-3 had drifted off to sleep, the Saphire family gathered under the open canopy. The sea slapped softly at the pontoons. It was the first meal they had shared since the world split apart.

Eisha ladled thin soup into metal cups and passed them around. Sam kept the radios beside him as always, their faint green lights steady. They were all back together again, but none of them wanted to tempt fate again.

For a while, they only listened to the waves. Then Sarah spoke.

"It started that afternoon," she said quietly. "Before the sky went wrong."

She'd been in her dorm room, reviewing notes for a marine biology exam. Outside, the wind had begun to rise—a low howl threading through window frames. Down the path, Sean, the Australian exchange student in the senior building, was also studying. Adam, meanwhile, was in the cafeteria, half watching the storm through the windows.

Then came the thunderous thump—the same one Sam and Eisha had heard miles away—the sound that cracked the sky open.

"Sean knew right away," Sarah said. "I heard him shouting for everyone to grab the floaters."

Sam frowned. "Floaters?"

"They built them after the smaller floods," Sarah explained. "Like lifeboats for each dorm. Sean helped design them. He didn't even grab his backpack—he just ran."

Rain hadn't just fallen that day; it attacked in sheets that behaved more like walls than water. Trees, streetlamps, cars—everything was being swept sideways in the torrent.

"He reached my building drenched," Sarah said, "and yelling, 'Top floors! Move!'"

She had been frozen by the window, watching the world tilt. Sean didn't hesitate—he grabbed her hand and dragged her toward the upper stairwell.

"I thought it would stop," she whispered. "Every other time, it had stopped. But this one didn't."

Adam leaned forward, face shadowed by the lantern. "I heard her scream," he said quietly. "Didn't even know where it came from."

He'd been helping friends load trays of bottled water when the cafeteria windows imploded. Cold surged inside instantly. He climbed onto a counter as the floor turned into a rising mirror.

"Sean told me everyone on campus would be in survival mode," Sarah said. "But all I could think about was Adam."

"I was fifty yards away," Adam said. "That's all. But the campus looked like the ocean had swallowed it whole."

On the top floor, students had already been dragging floaters into the hall—plastic-and-aluminum frames built to hold six to eight people. If the water reached them, they were meant to shove them straight out broken windows into the chaos below.

"I told Sean I had to find him," Sarah said.

Sean had grabbed her shoulders. "You stay with the others," he'd told her. "Help them launch. I'll find him."

She had hesitated, but Sean was already climbing through a blown-out stairwell window into the roar of wind.

Adam picked up the thread. "When the windows shattered, the water rushed in. I was holding onto a vending machine..." His voice faltered.

"Go on," Eisha murmured gently.

"Then these boats came through," Adam said. "Kids from the senior building. Sean was shouting my name. They pulled me out—I couldn't even feel my arms. The water was freezing, like needles all over my body. Sean dragged me into a floater and said, 'You're coming with me, mate.'"

They had reached Sarah's building just as the second surge hit. Inside, she cried with relief when Adam stumbled through the door.

"Sean didn't stay," she whispered. "He said more buildings needed help. He went back out before I could thank him."

Sam closed his eyes. "He saved both my children."

A third bombardment had rolled across the horizon—distant booms, nature's artillery. Anyone caught outside wasn't envied by those clinging to upper floors. The water did not retreat this time. It only rose, swallowing the landscape piece by piece.

Days had passed. Then weeks. The violent bursts eased, replaced by an endless, steady swell. Students who'd survived lashed floaters to roof fragments, solar panels, and even overturned staircases. People from nearby towns paddled over with whatever they had, drawn by instinct to cluster around human voices.

"Those floating towns just ... happened," Sarah said. "Accidentally at first. Then by design."

"For two months," Adam said, "we fought just to stay alive. Storms. Hunger. Cold. But there were nights when the sky was clear and full of stars." He looked past the rail toward the horizon, remembering. "Sometimes we'd talk about you," he said. "Wondering if you'd survived. And I'd tell Sarah about the neighbor's daughter across the street—the one I never spoke to." A faint smile tugged at him. "I kept thinking maybe she had survived somewhere, too."

Eisha touched his hand. "Love doesn't wait for logic," she said warmly.

Sarah laughed. "I learned that, too. Sean saved us both—and then vanished again. I hoped he'd come back."

As the waters steadied, they had joined a larger flotilla forming a proper settlement. Everyone brought what they knew—cooks, divers, teachers, builders.

"We had to start from nothing," Sarah said. "But it felt like the world was rebooting—and we got to write the first lines of code."

Radios had drowned long ago, but whenever they found a working one on another raft, they'd try it—calling out coordinates from memory, hoping someone somewhere was listening.

"We never stopped calling," Adam said.

Sarah nodded. "And one day, the relay crackled, and someone said there was a message—two names she couldn't pronounce: 'Sahf-air.' She said, 'If you hear this, they're looking for you.'"

"That was your signal," Eisha Eisha exhaled. "The one we sent from Rope Crown."

Adam nodded. "That was the moment. We just … knew."

The deck fell silent except for the soft push of the tide. Sam wiped his eyes with the back of his hand. Eisha brushed her fingers through Sarah's hair the same way she had when she was little.

"You were brave," she whispered. "Even braver than we taught you to be."

"We just did what you always told us," Sarah said. "When things fall apart, stick together and hold on."

Sam smiled faintly. "You remembered that."

"How could we forget?" Adam said. "That's what saved us."

They sat together, faces silvered by moonlight, radios humming softly beside them—four people finally tuned to the same frequency.

Later that night, long after the lanterns dimmed and Haven-3 quieted to the sigh of ropes and tide, Sam lingered by the comms deck. He wasn't expecting traffic; habit had trained his fingers to hover near the dials. The stars were sharp, almost metallic, and the air carried the faint sweetness that comes only after a storm has wrung itself dry.

Then the signal window flickered. Three short. Two long. One short.

Sam straightened. It wasn't an echo of their own beacon. It was new.

He turned up the volume. Static hissed, then parted.

"... if anyone receives this, my name's Sean Donnelly. Searching for survivors from University Southeast... Convoy drifted northwest... Coordinates unknown... I repeat—"

The transmission fractured, the voice dissolving into the sea.

Sam stared at the receiver for a long time before whispering, barely audible even to himself, "Sarah is going to want to hear this."

***

Outside, the horizon glowed with the first faint suggestion of dawn—a soft, forgiving line of light. The world was still shifting.

But now, for the first time in a long time, it was shifting toward possibility.

The following evening, after supper and cleanup and the effortless slipping of Haven-3 into its nighttime hush, the Saphire family gathered again beneath the open canopy. A gentle breeze carried the scent of salt and wet rope. Lanterns burned low to save power, casting warm halos over their faces.

Sam leaned back, arms crossed loosely, a quiet smile tugging at his mouth. "So," he said to Adam, "did you come up with any new theories while you were floating around out there?"

Sarah snorted before her brother could respond. "Oh, yes. He developed the theory of falling hopelessly in love with someone he's never spoken to."

Adam groaned. "Very funny."

Eisha grinned. "I read that paper."

Sam lifted an eyebrow. "You've always had a mind for speculation, son."

Adam stared up at the stars, the sky reflecting softly in his eyes. "Actually … I did think about a few things."

Sarah groaned dramatically. "Here we go…"

Adam ignored her teasing, his voice turning thoughtful. "I kept thinking about black holes—how a star grows weak, expands, and then collapses into one. It's strange, isn't it? Stars lose mass as they burn. They get lighter, more diffuse. So, how does something formed from a star that's shed most of its mass end up creating the strongest gravity in the universe?"

Sam tilted his head. "Go on."

"Well," Adam continued, sketching shapes in the air with his hands, "I know scientists say the collapse happens because the core becomes unstable—whatever that means—and that the extreme gravity comes from packing a huge amount of mass into a very tiny space. But that still doesn't explain why the collapse starts. If gravity comes from matter twisting the fabric of space, then as a star loses mass, its 'twist' on the fabric should weaken, not strengthen."

He paused, searching for the right words.

"I think the collapse comes from the fabric of space itself—untwisting."

Eisha blinked. "Like ... space pulling back?"

"Exactly," Adam said. "I call it the Space Untwisting Event."

Sam leaned forward, intrigued. "So, you're saying the fabric of space has its own strength? A kind of structural tension we could measure?"

"Maybe." Adam's smile was shy but confident. "Think about Einstein—$E = mc^2$. At the moment of equilibrium, right before the collapse, c is constant, and the star's mass can be estimated. So, the energy at that equilibrium point might represent the strength of the space fabric itself. The universe's resistance. Its backbone."

Sarah's eyes widened. "So, Einstein's E in $E = mc^2$ becomes zero inside a black hole, because no light, no matter?"

Adam exhaled, thinking. "Hmm... I don't know."

Eisha shook her head in wonder. "Only in this family do we end the day talking about the elasticity of the cosmos."

Sam looked at his children—alive, scarred, resilient—and felt something settle in him—something that had been trembling for months.

"Why don't you study astrophysics?" he asked Adam softly. "You think like a theorist."

Adam flushed. "Maybe someday. Right now, it's just ... homemade science. Ideas that float around in my head."

"They're interesting ideas," Eisha said.

Adam shrugged. "Maybe. They kept me calm when the world was falling apart."

Sarah nudged him affectionately. "And they kept me sane, listening to you."

Sam chuckled. "Stars and love," he said. "Some constants don't change."

They all laughed lightly, the sound drifting into the quiet.

Beyond them, the sea rocked Haven-3 in its slow tidal cradle. Lanterns swayed. The faint green glow of the radios pulsed like tiny, defiant constellations.

Above them, the real constellations shimmered—familiar shapes reclaimed from chaos, steady and bright. For the first time since the flood, the Saphire family wasn't simply surviving the world's transformation. They were part of its new beginning.

The Real and the Imaginary

Mornings in Haven-3 had begun to resemble something like normal life—whatever "normal" meant in a world rescued from extinction. The sun no longer barged through wounded clouds like a restless intruder. Instead, it warmed the floating walkways and rooftops gently, the way light once drifted across porches after a summer rain. A soft, salt-tinged breeze moved through the settlement most mornings, carrying the distant clatter of tools, the creak of shifting mooring lines, and the occasional bark of a dog someone had managed to rescue. And the sea—endless, patient, once terrifying—now breathed in steady, reassuring exhales beneath them. Its rhythm had softened into something like acceptance.

For the Saphire family, the world was no longer something to flee. It was something to understand. A new chapter had begun—not one of fear, but of curiosity.

Haven-3's registry had grown far beyond its improvised beginnings. What had once been a cluster of battered radios and handwritten lists had evolved into a delicate but impressive communications mesh. Solar beacons winked on the horizon. Relay drones hopscotched signals across miles of sparkling water. Every day at dawn, as sunlight spilled over the pontoons in pale gold sheets, the first sounds of the day were never alarms, only the quiet crackle of the morning broadcast. People paused with spoons in midair, listening in gentle silence to weather reports, drone paths, convoy updates, emergency pings, and the daily "Found and

Seeking" list. The soft voices from the mesh felt like the pulse of a slowly healing body.

Eisha tended the hydroponic trays each morning. The work carried a rhythmic peace—the hum of pumps, the soft rustle of leaves, the scent of fresh water and sprouting life. Sam coordinated scientific reports between flotillas, often working on shaded decks with his tablet propped against a coil of rope, the sea glittering in calm waves behind him.

Adam and Sarah spent their afternoons at the People's Mesh Hub, working silently at parallel terminals, immersed in survivor lists and signal maps. The hum of electronics and the gentle tapping of keys blended into a kind of meditative quiet. For the siblings, the Mesh Hub was where their new mission began—not survival, but reunion.

Adam rarely spoke about his search. But sometimes, when a packet from the Old Coast scanned through, he would pause, hands hovering, breath briefly held.

Sarah was more transparent. Every few transmissions, she leaned toward an operator and asked, "Any movement from the university flotilla? ... Any traffic from the south ridge convoy today? ... Any Australian signatures on long-range relays?"

The older operators teased her gently, never unkindly: "Still tracking your hero? ... Any word from that cowboy of yours?"

Sarah would redden, pretending to inspect a screen, and mutter, "Just checking."

Behind her, Adam smirked without looking up.

Behind Adam, Sam watched with a father's quiet amusement.

Eisha whispered once, "Let them chase. Dreams are rich soil for young hearts."

***

By midsummer, drones had become the arteries of the new world. Their soft whirring greeted each morning like birdsong. They carried letters, memory drives, seeds, small medical kits, and even a kitten someone insisted on delivering across three flotillas. Children imitated them with handmade toys, tracing them across the sky with squeals of delight. Sometimes the whole settlement paused to watch a large courier craft drift overhead, its belly filled with supplies, casting a slow-moving shadow like a quiet blessing.

Far beyond Haven-3, the western highlands—those peaks above 450 meters that had survived the flood—had become the beating heart of the Western Union of the Americas. The remnants of Colorado, Utah, and Arizona formed a scattered constellation of mountaintop cities. Communications towers perched on ridgelines, solar valleys glistened in the high-altitude sunlight, and hydro farms clung to cliffs. At night, long mountain corridors glowed faintly, stubborn defiance against the dark. What began as a coalition of exhausted engineers and surviving military bases had blossomed into a functioning civilization whose distant presence felt like an anchor. Haven-3 received its evening broadcast at dusk, when orange light pooled across the water like molten glass. The message always ended with *"Together, we rise again."* The words lingered as people settled in for the night, a lullaby more than a slogan.

One bright morning, the sea lay flat as polished glass. Adam knelt beside a silver beetle-shaped drone he had repaired with scavenged parts. He checked the antenna, tightened a bolt, and smoothed his thumb over the letters he'd etched by hand: SAPHIRE-H3-SEARCH-01. It carried a single data packet, a query about survivors from their old neighborhood.

He lifted it gently and released it. The drone rose with a faint shimmer, humming as it drifted into the blue.

Sarah leaned on the railing beside him. "Still chasing your ghost girl?" she teased.

Adam didn't look up. "Still waiting on your Australian cowboy?"

She elbowed him. He smirked.

The drone vanished into the horizon.

That evening, after chores, the youth of Haven-3 gathered near the docks. Warm lantern light pooled over the planks as the tide whispered beneath them. They traded stories of drifting flotillas, rumored outposts, and new water-frontier legends. There were tales of "rogue towns"—ragged communities floating lawless beneath tattered flags—and rumors of government patrols—"sea sheriffs"—bringing order, rescuing convoys, hunting raiders.

"I heard this one sheriff has a twenty-boat posse," a boy said dramatically.

"Strikes like lightning," another added.

"He's got an accent," a girl chimed in.

"Probably Australian."

Sarah rolled her eyes a beat too fast. Her stomach fluttered.

These stories seeded her quiet night prayers. Sometimes she imagined Sean steering through rain and thunder, lantern swinging in his cabin, calling her name through the static. Adam carried the opposite—a tenderness for a girl he barely remembered more than knew. Two kinds of longing. Two types of hope.

***

The next morning, as golden light draped Haven-3, Sarah's wrist comm vibrated. The sound cut through the stillness.

"This is Frontier Command—Haven East relay," came the voice. *"Message for Sarah Saphire from Sean Donnelly, coordinator of Rescue District Twelve. Priority channel."*

The family fell silent.

"Go ahead," Sam said gently.

The message scrolled:

Sarah,

Word of your family's survival reached us through the west relay.

Haven-3's rebuilding has inspired many here.

We stabilized our flotilla into a rescue hub.

We've recovered dozens of survivors.

People call me "the sheriff," which still feels strange.

If all goes well, I'll visit Haven-3 before the next relay cycle.

91

There's much to share—and something I'd like to say in person.

— Sean

Sarah read it twice, then again, covering her mouth.

Adam grinned. "Your daydream just filed a report in triplicate."

Sarah flushed.

"Maybe imagination was just … delayed," she whispered.

Sam nodded. "Discovery takes time."

Eisha squeezed her daughter's hand.

Adam looked away toward the quiet horizon. A soft ache rose in him—hope, envy, and something he couldn't name. He hid it behind a small smile.

For a long moment, the family stood together in the soft morning light, listening to the calm lap of the sea. No one hurried. Peace settled over them like a shawl.

That evening, the sky stretched into coral, apricot, and rose, like a promise the world was quietly trying to keep. Drones hummed overhead, their lights drifting in gentle arcs across the settling dusk.

Sarah and Adam stood on the observation deck. Below them, Lights glimmered across Haven-3 like scattered constellations, their reflections trembling softly with each swell.

"You fell for someone real—your feelings make sense," Adam said softly. "I fell for a dream. I can't explain mine."

"Maybe dreams are real," Sarah replied. "They just take longer to arrive."

Adam chuckled. "You sound like Dad."

He turned his gaze to the glowing horizon.

"The explicable and the inexplicable," he murmured. "Two sides of the same thing."

Behind them, Sam and Eisha lingered at the top of the stairs. Sam slipped his hand into Eisha's as they watched their children—older, wiser, yet still carrying wonder. The silence between them felt sacred. The world had changed, but humanity—messy, curious, hopeful—remained intact.

Later, as Sarah and Adam walked toward their moored family boat—the place they now called home—a soft breeze ruffled their hair. She noticed the distant look on her brother's face and nudged him.

"So," she said, "any new kitchen-table physics tonight?"

He smiled faintly. "Maybe. Pick: math, physics, or philosophy."

"Surprise me."

"Okay… I've been thinking about instantaneity."

"Instanti-what?"

Adam snorted. "Do you want to listen, or do you want to listen?"

She folded her arms. "Proceed, Professor."

"It's about moments happening all at once," he explained. "I heard a physicist say once that if we could travel to the nearest star at extreme speeds, we'd reach it in minutes—but millions of years would pass back home."

Sarah blinked. "Time dilation."

"Right. So, if we can't reach anything instantly—if everything we see is old light—then nothing far away is truly real in our time. Everything past a certain distance is just memory. Ghosts of what once was."

Sarah grimaced. "So ... we're the center of the universe?"

Adam shrugged. "Not the universe. Maybe just our bubble of time."

She groaned dramatically. "You know we could've used this time to fix the entire apocalypse, right?"

Adam laughed. "Mocking my brilliance again."

They both smiled. The night breeze was soft around them.

That night, while the settlement settled into bedtime quiet, Adam returned to the Mesh Hub. Only a few lanterns glowed inside. The hum of equipment was gentle, almost soothing.

He typed: *To anyone from the Old Coast neighborhoods— If you knew a girl named Rachelle ... tell her Adam Saphire is looking for her. We made it. I hope she did, too.*

He hesitated, then pressed send.

Outside, dozens of drones lifted into the night, their lights weaving slow, peaceful trails over the dark ocean, each carrying messages, dreams, and fragile hopes.

Somewhere out there, perhaps, someone would hear. But the search—the explicable and the inexplicable... It was far from over.

New New York

A year had taught the world to breathe in water.

Haven-3 no longer looked like a cluster of survivors clinging to luck; it pulsed like a city discovering its own heartbeat. Gardens grew in vertical tubes, bright with beans, herbs, and spinach. The old basketball court had become the town square, where children played and adults gathered for the nightly broadcast. Salt-bleached tarps had transformed into awnings over market stalls. The radio tower—once just a piece of salvaged rigging—now beamed out the one government channel that still stitched the scattered world together. "Report, repair, ration, respond"—the four R's had become scripture.

Sam Saphire—the scientist the children still called Dad and the people now called Doc—spent his days at the hydro-lab, switching between pumps and filtration readouts. But every night, after his shift, after the generators dimmed and the walkways quieted, his eyes drifted east.

Beyond the horizon lay Lebanon. His parents. His siblings. His nephews and nieces. Whole constellations of memory.

Every night, he tried to picture what had survived above the waves. Every night, he failed. The ocean had swallowed too much, and imagining what was left was like guessing the shape of a sunken cathedral.

One evening, after finishing his rounds, he unfolded a worn map, the paper soft as cloth from years of handling, and set it on the table between him and Eisha.

"I need to go," he said. Not with drama. Not with desperation. Just the quiet, immovable certainty of someone who had carried a question too long.

Eisha held his gaze. She saw the weight in his shoulders, the longing beneath the scientist's calm.

"You'll go with Adam?" she asked, though she already knew.

"Yes. He's ready."

A pause.

"And we'll travel by the registered lanes. We'll stop in New New York first—get clearance for the Great Crossing. The government is opening routes again."

Eisha exhaled slowly. "Then go. But go slow. And come home, Sam."

Their daughter, Sarah—now knee-deep in Haven-3's floating school and hydroponic gardens—tried to look brave, though the tightness around her eyes betrayed her. "We'll keep Haven-3 running. We'll have a home waiting when you're back."

The three of them held one another. It was an embrace heavy with salt, fear, and faith.

***

At dawn the next morning, the *Sea Glass* waited at the dock. She was a stubborn vessel—broad-bellied and welded from the bones of two old trawlers—and she rode the water with the confidence of a creature that had already survived storms.

Barlow, her captain, was already laughing before anyone spoke.

"You the professor?" he asked Sam, gripping his hand in a handshake that felt like testing the integrity of steel.

"Yes," Sam said.

"Good! Every ship needs one man who overthinks. I balance the equation by not thinking at all." He slapped the rail and roared with laughter, as if the joke had held the world together for decades.

Adam followed Sam up the gangway, taking in the scraped decks, the patched sails, the improvised solar panels strapped along the stern. He tried to swallow the knot in his throat. Leaving Haven-3 was more complicated than he had expected. But this was necessary. For Sam. For all of them.

They set off under a sky polished clean by wind. Haven-3 shrank behind them until its radio tower was just a thin spire against the horizon.

The ocean they sailed through was not the one their grandparents had known. Whole towns drifted now, lashed together by rope, sheet metal, and stubbornness. They passed families fishing from the upper windows of drowned houses. They saw rooftops converted into gardens, laundry lines strung between old chimneys, and flags stitched from repurposed tarps.

A cluster of makeshift platforms drifted by, children clambering over nets and ropes. A woman in patched goggles taught a class of kids how to splice a line properly. Adam smiled despite himself. It reminded him of Sarah, her determination to make the world better one tiny system at a time.

Sam watched him. "You okay?"

Adam nodded. "Just … thinking she'd love all this."

Sam gave a knowing little exhale. "She chose to stay. I think she wanted more time with the Haven-3 kids—and your mom's guess, maybe staying close to Sean." He placed a hand on Adam's shoulder. "She'll hear every detail." Adam chuckled softly.

Then came the warning from the government band:

"Tropical anomaly forming northeast. Adjust course ten degrees west."

Barlow glanced at his compass and scoffed. "Ten degrees west'll push us straight into the ridge current. Nah. We'll ride the flank. She's just wind wearing makeup."

Sam frowned. "The storms haven't behaved like the old models in months. They're—"

"Inexplicable," Barlow finished. "I know, Professor. But the sea and I, we have an understanding."

Adam whispered to Sam, "That's not very comforting."

Sam whispered back, "It shouldn't be."

By afternoon, the sky bruised green. The temperature dropped as if the air had inhaled too sharply. Wind gathered in strange bursts—slamming one moment, falling silent the next. The *Sea Glass* groaned like a warning.

Then the storm hit. Waves rose like cliffs. Wind screamed as rain defied gravity, slamming sideways into the hull, testing the boat's grip on its line. The sky flickered with pale lightning that flashed from cloud to cloud. Thunder cracked like the splitting of continents.

"Keep her nose to the wind!" Barlow bellowed. "Don't let her turn broadside!"

Sam tied down a fuel drum with trembling hands. Adam tried to hold a tarp in place, but was thrown back against the rail, wind knocking the breath from his lungs.

Suddenly, a wall of water rose higher than the boat's mast and crashed across the deck. Adam stumbled, nearly losing his footing. Sam lunged and grabbed his arm, pulling him back from the edge.

"Stay with me!" Sam yelled over the roar.

"I'm trying!"

Barlow wrestled the helm with the fierce, tender focus of someone protecting an old friend. The *Sea Glass* groaned, but held.

Hours passed—long, twisting hours in which time existed only in heartbeats and the next wave. At one point, Adam turned pale, grabbed the rail, and emptied everything he had left in his stomach. Sam rubbed his back, steadying him.

"You're doing well," he said.

"You're lying," Adam croaked.

"Yes," Sam admitted. "But with love."

Even in terror, they found a sliver of warmth.

Finally, as dawn bled through the clouds, the waves grew long and slow as the raging breath of the storm softened.

Barlow spat into the wind triumphantly. "Ha! Told you she was only flirting!"

Sam collapsed to the deck, soaked and trembling. "*That* was flirting?"

Barlow winked. "The sea doesn't kill those she likes."

Adam shook his head. "Next time, she likes someone else."

***

Three days later, low on food and fuel, they sighted a massive dome breaking the water's surface—the half-sunken roof of an old stadium. Around it, barges were chained together like a rough necklace. The banner stretched across the largest barge read, RED HARBOR.

Adam scanned with binoculars. "No sheriff-patrol signal."

"Means the law's local," Barlow muttered. "So, try not to look edible."

The docks were lined with men and women who looked sculpted from rust and desperation. Their wetsuits were stitched with rope. Their belts sparkled with mismatched knives. Their eyes were hollow with hunger and suspicion.

The leader, a tall woman with a shaved head and mirrored glasses, sauntered forward with a smile that tried too hard.

"Travelers pay to dock. Supplies for supplies. No exceptions."

Barlow spread his arms theatrically. "Lady, we're here to buy trouble, not rent it. Let's talk food and fuel."

The crowd murmured.

Someone muttered, "Why trade?"

Another answered, "Cut the drifters' throats. Take their loot."

Sam noticed Adam inching closer to him, hand grazing the strap of their pack.

A boy, thin as a shadow, darted forward and tugged at Adam's shoulder strap.

"Hey!" Adam snapped, jerking back.

The boy's hand came back empty, but the attempt was enough. The crowd surged.

A man shoved Sam, almost sending him over the edge. Barlow's knife flashed instantly—not to strike, but as a warning.

The woman drew a homemade gun, its barrel crooked but lethal.

Then Barlow roared, a sound like a storm breaking open from inside his chest. It echoed across the docks, silencing breath and movement.

"STOP!"

The knives stilled. The dog behind the crates went quiet. Even the breeze hung motionless for a heartbeat.

"If we had anything worth stealing," Barlow shouted, "we wouldn't be stopping here! We've got nothing but salt in our bones and too many damn stories!"

The silence held. Then the woman snorted.

"Old man has a point. Let 'em rest. No trades. You leave before dawn."

And just like that, the tension unraveled into a strange, brittle hospitality. Crates became chairs. Rum appeared in chipped cups. A barrel fire hissed in the damp air.

Barlow launched into tales immediately—tales of whales the size of skyscrapers, storms that swallowed moons, mermaids that ran gambling dens. The raiders laughed, drawn into the performance.

Sam smiled politely. Adam played along. But beneath their expressions, both stayed alert.

When most of Red Harbor had fallen into a drunken stupor, Barlow leaned in.

"Soon," he whispered.

They slipped through the shadows between crates and makeshift stalls. The smell of stale liquor, engine oil, and rotting nets pressed thick around them.

A dog lifted its head, eyes glinting. A growl rumbled.

Adam froze. Sam stiffened.

Barlow slowly reached into his pocket and tossed a strip of dried fish. The dog sniffed ... then padded away.

But footsteps approached.

A pirate staggered from behind a broken generator, rubbing his eyes. He spotted Barlow's silhouette and squinted.

"You again... The loud one..."

Barlow lurched forward, performing an exaggerated drunken wobble. "That rum tasted like vinegar!"

The pirate barked a laugh, slapped his shoulder, and wandered off.

Sam exhaled slowly. "That was too close."

"Bah," Barlow muttered. "He's too drunk to remember his own name."

Then a soft shuffle came from the dark.

A child—thin, silent, maybe ten—stood half-hidden between stacked fuel drums, watching them.

For a moment, none of them moved.

Then the boy lifted a finger and pointed deeper into the maze of crates.

No words—just a look that said there.

Barlow nodded once, as if acknowledging an old ritual, and led the way.

Behind the crates lay a stash: fuel canisters, coiled cables, ration tins—piled in a haphazard, guilty mound.

The kind of hoard taken from drifters who never returned.

Sam swallowed. Adam looked away.

But they didn't have a choice.

They took only what they needed—fuel, cables, a few tins—moving quickly under the boy's watchful eyes. Then they slipped back toward the *Sea Glass*..A bottle shattered behind them. A dog barked. A voice swore.

They didn't look back.

Gunfire cracked once, twice—but their boat was already cutting toward open water.

Barlow laughed at the helm. "Don't worry. They'll sober up just in time to rob each other."

Sam shook his head in disbelief.

Adam muttered, "We owe that man our lives."

"More like our sanity," Sam said.

But the truth was more profound: Barlow had become undeniably important.

Once they were a safe distance from Red Harbor, Sam switched to the government band, searching for a clean frequency window. Static hissed, glitched, then cleared.

"Eisha? Can you hear me?"

A heartbeat. Then—

"Sam!"

Her voice—thin, distant, beautiful.

"Adam! Are you safe?"

Relief hit Sam so hard, his knees almost buckled.

"We survived a storm and out-drank pirates," he said breathlessly.

Eisha laughed, the sound bright even through the distortion. *"You two sound like teenagers."*

Barlow called from behind them, "Tell her the captain's single!"

Sarah's laughter burst through the background.

Adam leaned in close to the mic. "Mom, you'd love our captain—he's insane."

"We'll talk when you get home," Eisha said softly. *"Come back in one piece. All of you."*

The signal faded, but the warmth lingered. Sam inhaled deeply, feeling something he hadn't felt in a long time.

Hope.

***

They reached a floating refueling station late in the week—three barges welded into a horseshoe shape, humming with generators and the chatter of crews repairing nets and engines.

Barlow met the two of them on the pier, kicking at a loose rope like a man reluctant to say goodbye.

"This is where we part," he said, gripping Sam's hand. "From here, you fly."

Sam pulled him into an unexpected hug. "You kept us alive."

Barlow stepped back, eyes twinkling. "No, Professor. The sea let you pass. I just argued with her when she got moody."

Adam laughed. "We'll look for you on the way back."

Barlow pointed a finger at them. "And you'd better have stories worth hearing."

He turned, coat flapping like a banner of defiance, and disappeared into the crowd of dockworkers.

For a long moment, Sam and Adam watched the place where he had stood.

"It's hard to explain," Adam murmured, "but I feel safer knowing he's out there."

Sam nodded. "Some people make the world less lonely just by existing."

They boarded the amphibious shuttle—an awkward but surprisingly stable craft, assembled from welded jet components and buoyant pontoons. Its engines hummed like an old memory waking. The craft shuddered, water spraying along its sides, then lifted—slowly, trembling, fighting gravity.

Adam gripped the armrests, knuckles white. Sam's breath caught in his throat. It was the first time they had flown since the flood.

Below them, the ocean stretched in undulating blues and greens. Sunlight rippled across submerged highways like silver veins. The tops of drowned towers cut the water's surface like the ribs of forgotten beasts.

"Look…" Adam pointed out.

They stared at the ghost of the old world beneath them. Entire neighborhoods blurred by water, the faint grid of streets visible only when the light struck just right.

"The world's still here," Adam said. "Just rearranged."

Sam swallowed. "Adaptation is a kind of forgiveness."

A cluster of floating towns drifted beneath them—rafts tethered to rooftops, windmills spinning, gardens glowing under makeshift greenhouse domes. Sam saw a group of children laughing on a tilted rooftop, chasing a drone that dipped low like a playful bird. A woman waved at the shuttle from a tower balcony.

Life was stubborn. Life refused to drown.

***

At sunrise, the city appeared.

New New York rose from the water like a dream made of steel and grief. Towers—those that had survived the floods—pierced the surface. They were crowned with solar sails, gardens, landing pads, and greenhouse domes. Between them, a lattice of walkways and pontoons shimmered in the golden light. Helicopters zipped between platforms. Cargo drones skimmed the waves. Divers moved beneath the surface, carrying tools and sealed crates. The ocean around the city glowed with colors—reds, blues, greens, like an aurora trapped in water.

But the most arresting sight was beneath. Through the glassy surface, Sam and Adam could see the drowned city below—the skeletal frames of skyscrapers, the faint outlines of old streets. Sam felt his breath catch.

"We didn't abandon the city. We just... flipped it."

The pilot pointed with pride. "We call her the Waterfield. Still the heart of the States."

They docked at Harbor One, a vast floating platform attached to the side of a tower. A man in government blue waved glowing paddles. A crisp flag snapped overhead: UNITED EARTH – HOLD THE LINE.

When the engines cut, the world fell suddenly quiet except for waves and turbines.

A young officer approached. "Dr. Saphire? Rafi sent word ahead, said you'd be coming."

Sam blinked. "Rafi? He—you got his message?"

The officer smiled. "That man has friends everywhere. You'll be staying with Eli and Noor Harbad—engineers from Boston

107

Sector. They've got a deck apartment on H-17. Dry, wired, stable. You'll have space to rest, eat, and prepare for the Great Crossing."

Sam laughed. "Rafi's still pulling strings."

"His exact words," the officer said, "were, 'Make their landing soft.'"

The tower's interior smelled of machine oil, warm bread, and ozone. Walkways buzzed with activity—welders repairing railings, children carrying crates of seedlings, radio units barking announcements in overlapping languages.

Their hosts opened the door to H-17 with warm smiles.

Eli Harbad was short and silver-haired, his jumpsuit stained with grease. Noor was taller, her hands dusted with flour, her eyes deep and calm.

"So, these are the travelers from Haven-3," Noor said. "Rafi warned me you'd arrive half-dead and starving."

Sam sagged into a chair. "We've had ... quite a week."

"Then you eat," she said simply. "The sea takes enough. It doesn't get to take your supper, too."

She served fresh bread still warm from a compact solar oven, olives preserved in jars, and steaming tea that smelled like home.

Adam bit into the bread and closed his eyes. "This tastes like real life."

"It is real life," Eli said. "Or our version of it."

Sam smiled. "Thank you. Truly."

"You'll help where you can," Eli said. "Everyone does. But tonight—rest."

They did.

***

Sam and Adam spent a week in New New York, absorbing the rhythm of a city that refused to die. Sam accompanied Eli on maintenance rounds. Together, they checked pressure seals on underwater airlocks. Inspected algae-powered batteries. Repaired a jammed turbine blade that hummed like a heartbeat. Mapped pressure readings in submerged corridors. Sam marveled at human ingenuity. Every tower was a hybrid of old skyscraper architecture and new marine engineering.

Eli laughed once when Sam recoiled from a surge of warm water.

"Relax, Doc. That's just the desalination line burping. Means it's working."

Sam took notes on everything—ideas he could bring back to Haven-3.

Adam spent much of his time in the hydroponic labs. The algae tanks fascinated him—how they glowed when stirred, how they powered lighting lines underwater, how the divers used bioluminescent strands to signal in dark tunnels.

A teenage apprentice named Mira taught him how they harvested nutrient gel. She was patient, direct, and had Sarah's same stubborn curiosity.

"You're good at this," she said one day.

Adam shrugged. "My sister would be better."

"You'll tell her about us?"

"Everything," he said.

At night, they drank tea with their hosts, listening to radios murmuring in Arabic, French, Amharic, Bengali. Children laughed on the walkways while turbines hummed like a distant lullaby.

Sam often stood at the porthole, watching the lights dance on the water. He found himself thinking about the title Adam had once given his homemade theories: the explicable and the inexplicable. The world right now was exactly that—half science, half miracle.

***

One evening, as the sun bled gold over the waves, the loudspeakers crackled.

"This is Central Earth Coordination. Great Crossing registry opens at dawn. Report, repair, ration, respond."

Sam stared east.

"Now that we've rested," he said quietly, "we cross."

Adam nodded. "To Lebanon."

The lights of New York flickered like hope scattered across the water.

That night, after Adam fell asleep, Sam sat at the porthole. He opened his tablet, fingers trembling slightly, and typed:

Eisha, Sarah—

We made it.

New York is alive, Eisha. Not the way it was, but alive all the same. The towers glow like lanterns above the sea. Below them lies the ghost of the old world—still, silent, waiting. People here refuse to give up. Divers salvage parts from the drowned subway lines. Kids chase drones across floating walkways. Engineers patch towers with nothing but recycled bolts and hope.

The world is wounded, but it breathes.

Tell everyone in Haven-3: we're still part of a story worth fighting for.

Hold the line.

Love,

Sam

He hit send. The signal light blinked—once, twice—then steadied. He leaned back, letting the gentle sway of the tower lull him.

Bread was baking somewhere down the corridor. Voices hummed. Life persisted.

For the first time in months, Sam slept without listening for the wind—without bracing for the storm that might follow..

The Great Crossing

In the morning, they reached the port, and the air carried the mixed scent of diesel, salt, metal, and new beginnings. The eastern docks of New New York were a fever of motion—ropes whipping against cleats, cranes swinging overhead, generators thumping, workers calling across the chaos like a city resurrecting itself one shouted instruction at a time. The sky was a crisp silver-blue, the kind that made everything feel slightly sharpened, as if the world itself had been honed during the night.

Sam and Adam walked the length of the harbor with duffel bags slung over their shoulders, stepping around coils of rope and crates stamped with the new world's patchwork symbols. Boats of every kind crowded the waterfront: sailboats reborn as ferries, fishing trawlers refitted into cargo lifelines, catamarans plastered with solar panels like mirrored scales. Amphibious shuttles skimmed the water's edge and lifted into the air on bursts of spray, forming arcs of sunlit mist. Sheriffs in blue vests moved among the docks with clipboards and earpieces, their calm authority grounding the cacophony in something that felt like order.

Above the main pier, a sign hung with the boldness of a proclamation: GREAT CROSSING CONVOY — REGISTRY & BRIEFING. The line of travelers stretched almost to the seawall— families clutching bundles, engineers lugging toolboxes, divers with oxygen tanks slung over their backs, scientists murmuring quietly among themselves. A few faces wore an expression Sam recognized from the early days at Haven-3, carved from

113

stubbornness, braced against fear, committed to change even when the cost was unclear.

The loudspeakers announced departure windows in a voice that was both mechanical and strangely maternal.

"Convoy East—departure at dawn. Hulls One through Twenty: prepare for final inspection. Report, repair, ration, respond."

Sam felt the tension in Adam's shoulders beside him. The boy—no, the young man—stood tall, but his eyes scanned everything, absorbing details the way only someone who had survived chaos could.

"First time seeing a place like this," Adam murmured, "where people aren't running from something—they're running toward something."

Sam nodded, though the line between the two had often blurred.

Their hosts, Noor and her husband, Eli, had arranged everything for them before leaving for the southern routes. Their convoy card read HULL #17—a midline vessel, not too large, but not too fragile. A sheriff inspected their credentials, stamped their card, and waved them toward the staging platform.

Sam had barely taken a step when he froze. At the far end of the dock stood a figure unmistakable even in silhouette—broad shoulders, a storm-weathered coat, boots scuffed by decades of salt, and a beard that could have been carved from driftwood.

Captain Barlow.

He turned at the same moment Sam did, laughter erupting from him before a single word could form.

"Well, I'll be damned if it isn't my favorite science experiment and his boy!"

"Barlow?" Sam blinked as if the man might vanish like a mirage. "You're … commanding one of these ships?"

"One of?" Barlow barked out a laugh that boomed over the noise of the docks. "The one and only! Hull Seventeen. That's ours." He jabbed a thumb over his shoulder toward a vessel that looked equal parts wounded and proud, solar sails folded like steel dragonfly wings, hull striped with welded scars that glinted in the sun. "Name's still *Sea Glass*. She's uglier than ever and twice as stubborn."

Adam broke into a grin he hadn't felt since leaving Haven-3. "You knew we'd be coming?"

"I knew you'd try," Barlow said, the grin softening in a way that made him look younger, almost gentle. "The minute I heard about the Great Crossing, I thought, 'Those Saphires are the kind that chase the edge of the world. And the world's not done testing good men yet.'"

He clapped Sam on the shoulder hard enough to sting. "Couldn't let you cross this ocean alone. Besides, the storm we're heading into isn't for rookies. You'll need a madman who can smell bad water before it even thinks about turning."

Sam laughed despite himself, the tension melting from his spine. "You knew this would be dangerous."

"Everything worth doing is," Barlow said. Then, leaning close with a conspiratorial whisper, he said, "But between us, every time the sea tries to kill me, she ends up teaching me something instead. This trip? This'll be the master class."

Adam felt a flicker of joy—genuine, bright, rare. In a world rebuilt from loss, familiarity was treasure. Seeing Barlow again— this ragged, fearless captain who had laughed through storms and stared down pirates—felt like discovering a forgotten piece of the old world still afloat.

The convoy master barked orders from the tower, voice echoing over the water. Cranes swung like patient mechanical insects loading cargo onto deck after deck. The rising sun threw a red-gold sheen over the assembled fleet—forty-seven vessels lined up in disciplined anarchy under a shared flag:

UNITED EARTH – HOLD THE LINE

Barlow looked out across the glittering ocean, then back at them. "This is the one storm the world's been preparing for its whole life, boys. Not wind or water—change. And we're sailing straight through the center of it." He spat into the sea—an old sailor's pact. "Now, grab your gear, Professor. We've got an ocean to argue with."

Sam and Adam followed him up the gangway. For one moment—one precious moment—they felt something rare, like they were not alone. Hope threaded through their ribs like a pulse.

***

The *Sea Glass* left port at dawn, pushing off with the tide and a mild list to port, with the convoy card stamped, channels tested, and radars synced. They'd join the great chain in stages: New York Waterfield. Newfoundland Ridge. Isles Station. Azores Carrier. Iberian Spur. Sheriffs had briefed them: standardize channels, log cargo, settle disputes early, travel tight at dawn and dusk, go loose at noon when the glare made targeting difficult. The rest would be weather, luck, and will.

Luck arrived first.

For two days, the Atlantic unrolled like a clean ledger under a sky so bright, it felt close enough to touch. The ghost of the skyline lingered only in their memory now—needle points of a drowned city, their reflections scattered into trembling watercolor by the swells. The convoy quickly found its rhythm. Electric engines hummed under the solar drapes by day; at night, the gas motors whispered the low growl of combustion. The government channel clicked and murmured—*"window opens; window closes; sheriffs redeploy"*—keeping time like a metronome guiding an orchestra made of hulls and hope. Amphibs hopscotched overhead in short-range flight patterns, dipping their wings—a tiny salute to the ships below.

That night, Dr. Saphire woke with the visceral instinct that someone was standing over him.

A prickle ran up his spine before his eyes fully opened. The low creak of the hull, the distant slap of water, and then—breathing. Close—too close.

Sam rolled to his side instantly, hand closing around the wrench he kept by his bunk. A face stared back at him—gray-bearded, hollow-cheeked, eyes bright with a calm that was both unnerving and strangely lucid. His grin revealed more gaps than teeth.

Sam jolted upright, heart hammering. "Who the hell—"

The man lifted his palms slowly. "Easy, Doc. Not a thief. Just … a guest. You drifted into my neighborhood."

Adam burst in, barefoot, breath sharp. "Dad?" He froze at the sight of the stranger, then glanced at the porthole—where a strange amber light filtered through something dense.

Barlow's voice echoed from the helm. "Well, I'll be damned—looks like we've sailed into a landfill that decided to eat the horizon!"

They climbed onto the deck. What lay before them was not ocean; it was a continent of debris stretching farther than the horizon could swallow. Doors, nets, ruined barrels, mattresses, pieces of homes, hulls of boats, strangling vines of plastic, all floating in a thick, sun-bleached mat.

A world of forgotten things.

Barlow scratched his beard. "All right, I'll own it—I dozed off at the wheel. The current pulled us here. This stuff doesn't drift; it grows. Don't like the feel of it. But she's afloat … mostly."

The stranger exhaled softly. "Nobody sails here, Captain. They drift in. This place catches you the way grief does—quiet, accidental. Most people don't know they're trapped until the ocean's already decided to keep them."

Sam looked out over the sprawling mess, uneasy. "How many people live here?"

"Depends on what you call 'living.'" The man's voice was like a worn rope. "Some wash in after storms. Some scavenge and build nests. Some wait for new arrivals with hands out and knives behind their backs. A few of us try to help folks leave before the rest notice they've got something worth taking."

Calls echoed across the floating wasteland.

"Help us! Please! My baby—she's sick!"

"Trade! We can trade! Medicine! Fuel!"

Adam stiffened. Sam's breath caught. Barlow's jaw tightened.

"That's bait," the captain muttered.

The stranger nodded. "The moment you stop, you're theirs."

Shapes emerged among the debris—figures half-clothed, faces smeared in grime, moving with the hunger of people too long stranded between hope and cruelty. One leapfrogged onto a nearby plank, then another, edging closer with hollow smiles.

Barlow's voice cut through the air like a blade. "That's far enough!" He raised his revolver—old, polished by storms and care. "If we had anything worth stealing, we wouldn't be here."

The figures read the command in his tone. One hissed and retreated. Others melted into the maze of trash.

Sam turned to the remaining stranger. "Come with us. You don't have to stay … here."

The man smiled—a real one, fragile and warm. "If I leave, who warns the next poor soul how to get out? Somebody's got to stay and light a candle, even in a place that eats the flame."

Barlow tipped his head in respect. "Son, that's nobler than most sermons I've heard floating around."

The man pointed toward a seam in the debris, where the water shimmered a cleaner shade. "Head south by a hair. Quiet water. That's your door. Don't look back. Don't answer the calls."

Sam gripped his forearm. The drifter returned the gesture with surprising strength.

As the *Sea Glass's* engines sputtered to life, the stranger stood atop a broken roof beam. "Keep your line, Captain," he called out. "The ocean remembers those who forget to listen!"

The vessel began to crawl through the labyrinth, hull scraping against forgotten furniture and rusted appliances. They crept through the junk continent for nearly an hour, turning a deaf ear to the siren song of those they passed.

When the sea finally reemerged—dark, clean, endless—Barlow exhaled deeply. "We're out."

Sam glanced back. The stranger's raised arm—one final, heartfelt goodbye from a good Samaritan who had briefly felt like a friend—was the last thing he saw, an image that lingered long after the haze swallowed him..

Barlow turned to the console, scanning channels. "Convoy's out there. We drifted off course. Let's see who's awake enough to answer."

Static. Then a faint beacon—three slow pings, one fast.

"Hull Six," Barlow murmured. "Relay's intact."

Adam leaned over the railing. "Do you think he'll be okay?"

"That drifter?" Barlow said gently. "Some folks are born to stay put so others can keep going."

They caught up with the convoy by nightfall. But the real test still lay ahead.

***

They rejoined the convoy as the sky shifted toward violet. One ship appeared on the horizon, then another, until the wide ocean again held the familiar glow of scattered running lights, like a constellation drifting across the Atlantic. Voices crackled over the shared mesh, checking positions, swapping course corrections, offering quiet relief that the chain had not broken.

The following days settled into a pattern—work, watch, repair, rest. Sam found himself adjusting to the rhythm of the crossing. It reminded him of Haven-3, but rougher, more exposed, more honest. You learned a vessel the way you learned a person: by listening for the creaks that meant fatigue and the silences that meant danger.

Barlow lectured to the sky as much as the sea. "Clouds talk," he'd say, pointing at the shifting gray. "And when they stop talking, that's when you worry."

Adam soaked in every word, standing beside him at the helm during long stretches. Sam watched the two of them—Barlow's seasoned instinct paired with Adam's sharp mind—and felt a strange, quiet pride.

But the weather had its own agenda.

The first sign was the barometer—a subtle drop that deepened into a sullen plunge. The air thickened. The horizon turned sharp, its colors metallic. Birds vanished from the sky. Even the convoy chatter thinned, the unspoken understanding passing between captains: something big was stirring.

By the next morning, the wind shifted twice in an hour—never a good sign.

"Storm band forming," came a call over the mesh. *"No center yet. Choose: forward to outrun, or back to be beaten."*

Barlow was already at the helm, rain beginning to prick his beard. "Forward," he said without hesitation. "You don't dodge a storm. You teach it manners."

No vote was called. The ocean made autocrats of weather and democrats of those who wished to survive it.

They turned into the rising wind. The wall of cloud forming ahead wasn't a hurricane in the neat, circular sense. It was worse— a broken, seemingly endless chain of rotating cells, wild, uneven, unpredictable. Too large to skirt. Too fast to retreat from.

Barlow grinned into the wind as though greeting an old rival. "All right, girl," he murmured to the *Sea Glass*, "I know you hate theatrics. But let's dance."

The first waves lifted the bow with casual power, the way a giant might test the strength of a toy before deciding whether to snap it. Salt sprayed the deck, stinging eyes and raw knuckles.

"Bow up!" Barlow shouted. "Always bow up!"

Sam worked the pump, then the line, rotating with Adam in a practiced rhythm. Adam wedged himself into the engine space, checking the mounts and gauges as the *Sea Glass* shuddered.

Lightning cracked across the sky, spidering in unnatural patterns. Thunder rolled not in booms, but in layered growls, like the sky grinding its teeth.

When the worst came, the storm didn't announce it; it simply delivered it.

The world narrowed into a tunnel of water, gray and boiling. The *Sea Glass* climbed waves that felt like rushing hills, then dropped into troughs so deep that the horizon vanished completely.

"Hold!" Barlow roared, barefoot at the wheel, soaked and laughing in a way that felt half insane and half sacred. "The sea only kills whoever bows too low!"

A wall of water slammed into them broadside. Sam hit the deck hard, sliding until his shoulder struck the rail. Adam grabbed a support beam, arm muscles bunching like rigging lines. A crate of wire broke loose, skidding across the deck until two hands grabbed it—a deckhand and Sam together, straining as the hull rolled sickeningly.

"Pump!" Barlow barked. "Keep her lungs clear!"

Sam staggered and resumed pumping. Every stroke felt like wrestling the ocean itself.

The electric engines whined as spray soaked the sails. One gas motor sputtered. Adam cursed, slamming a fist against the housing, and the engine coughed back to life. It wasn't pretty, but it was obedient.

A voice over the mesh cut through the madness:

"Hull Twenty-One cracked—taking water—assistance needed."

Three boats peeled off to aid them. Even in chaos, the convoy instinct held: protect the wounded, close ranks, endure together. The storm didn't want victims; it wanted participants.

For hours, the *Sea Glass* rose and fell in a brutal rhythm. Sam felt each wave in his bones. The world became three commands repeated like scripture: *bow up, hold, pump. Bow up, hold, pump.*

And then, as suddenly as if a divine hand had released them, the wind eased. The rain softened. The horizon reappeared in faint, trembling strips of light.

Morning returned like a divine apology.

The convoy's voices rose across the mesh—injury counts, damage tallies, rough laughter, exhausted sighs. Two boats gone: one salvaged by a sheriff's tow, another reduced to debris, but its crew had been recovered. Four injuries: a broken arm splinted with a broom handle, a cracked rib, and two deep cuts. People had already begun turning the story into something mythic—humanity's natural instinct to translate pain into meaning.

Barlow leaned on the rail, soaked and triumphant. He spat into the calm water. "Ocean's got a temper," he said quietly. "But she respects effort. We gave her hell, and she decided not to eat us today."

Sam exhaled, letting the tension drain from his shoulders. Adam glanced at him, eyes red-rimmed but bright.

"You all right?" he asked.

Sam nodded. "You?"

Adam took a breath. "I was terrified," he admitted. "But … I wasn't frozen. Not like before."

Sam squeezed his shoulder. "That's what growth feels like—fear moving aside just enough for you to act."

Barlow grinned. "Look at that—Saphires having breakthroughs on my boat. Put that in the weather report."

For a fleeting hour, peace settled. The sun broke through. The air smelled cleaner.

Then, the engine died.

Not dramatically—no explosion, no plume of smoke. Just a choking cough, a metallic sigh, and silence.

Adam stared at the panel. "Dad … all our readings were green."

Sam's chest tightened. During the storm, he'd noticed a strange stutter in the fuel feed—a gauge that flickered once, then behaved. He'd dismissed it. They'd had no room for worry then.

Barlow tapped the console. "Storm math," he said soberly. "She's got her own bookkeeping. Salt water in the intake, probably. Maybe a cracked line."

They tried to restart. They bled the manifold, primed the injectors, coaxed, cursed, pleaded. Nothing.

Solar drapes were torn. Wind had shredded one of the charging lines. The electric pack gave them only a whisper of power.

They drifted. It was one thing to drift by choice, another entirely to drift as a verdict.

Sam tuned the radio and forced calm into his voice. "Hull Seventeen, dead in the water. No immediate danger. Coordinates are…" He read them off. "Requesting relay."

Silence.

Then static.

Faintly, the mesh crackled to life. *"Keep your line. Repeat: hold your line."*

But the voice vanished before they could reply.

Adam leaned against the railing, staring at the sky. "We survived the storm," he said softly. "And now this."

"Storms don't end when the wind stops," Sam said. "Sometimes the aftermath is the real test."

Barlow stood at the wheel, even though the wheel commanded nothing. "Patience," he muttered. "The waves take their time answering prayers."

***

Two hours later, salvation arrived not on the water, but above it.

An amphib broke through the clouds—sleek, silver, flying low. It circled once, then transmitted sharply:

"Seventeen, I read you. Relaying to Isles Station and Azores Carrier. Hold position. Help en route."

Barlow slapped the console. "See? Told you. Ocean listens to people who talk nicely."

Help came on a boat patched with more hope than metal. The Portuguese name on its stern read like a hymn. The crew wore the look of people who had seen much and complained little. They lashed alongside, exchanged greetings, traded tools and jokes. They opened the cowling and reached elbow-deep into the engine's stubborn heart.

"Stormwater," one said, shaking his head. "Clogged intake. Also, a crack here. Lucky."

"Lucky?" Adam muttered.

"Lucky it is fixable," the man offered, smiling.

Barlow worked beside them, sleeves rolled up, swearing in English, French, and something that might have been Portuguese. "You'll run, you old sinner," he said, tapping the intake. "You just needed attention. We all do."

When the engine caught—just a cough at first, then a healthy growl—the crew cheered like a stadium in miniature.

Sam exhaled, laughter breaking through his relief. Adam wiped his eyes, pretending it was salt spray.

Barlow threw back his head and laughed, water dripping from his beard. "See, Doc? The trick ain't fighting the sea—it's reminding her we belong here."

The repaired engine rumbled beneath them. The *Sea Glass* straightened, found her footing on the waves, and steered east with new confidence.

The convoy soon shimmered on the horizon, dotted with lights that felt almost like home.

Barlow nudged the throttle. "Europe's out there. She may not be the Europe we remember, but she's waiting."

Sam looked ahead. The horizon seemed both closer and impossibly far.

Adam leaned beside him. "Do you think Europe survived better than we did?"

Sam's answer was quiet, almost reverent. "We'll find out soon enough."

The *Sea Glass* pushed forward, the ocean—vast, ancient, and full of questions.

The Great Crossing was far from over. But they were moving again. And sometimes, in a world reborn from ruin, movement was enough.

Why the Journey?

For a week, the sea behaved as if it had made peace with them. Days opened slow and golden, the convoy stretched and tightened with the tide, and people finally spoke of arrival as a promise rather than a gamble. The *Sea Glass* rode smooth, solar wings humming, sails whispering, Captain Barlow whistling off-key as he steered by the sun and instinct.

Sam had stopped counting the days, until one morning, he realized it had been weeks since New New York had vanished behind them. It felt like a month and an hour all at once. The ocean was vast, yes, but so was the silence they had finally learned to inhabit.

By midday, the deck was warm enough to sit barefoot against the steel. Sam and Adam leaned against the railing, the convoy shimmering around them, each ship a floating speck of endurance.

Morning arrived like a promise no one dared to jinx: thin wind, low, even swells, sky rinsed clean. The convoy drifted loose at noon to spare nerves and fuel. Boats floated just within hailing distance, each one a patient dot on an endless sheet of blue glass.

Sam and Adam let the hush do half the talking.

The ocean went on forever. So did their reasons for the journey.

"You see it?" Sam said, nodding at the seam where water met sky. "That line. You can walk toward it all day; it never moves. Some things are like that."

"Which things?" Adam asked.

"Roots," Sam said, gazing towards Europe.

Silence settled again—comfortable, familiar. A flying fish startled the surface into glitter. Far off, an amphib skimmed the horizon before pulling back up into the sky. The hourly convoy check crackled on: *"hull number..., course..., good."* The solar drape fluttered sleepily, like a resting wing.

"Tell me," Adam said. "Not the facts. The why."

Sam smiled without taking his eyes off the water. "Because if I start with facts, I'll use them to hide," he agreed.

"Then don't."

He didn't.

"I grew up where the sea breezes smell like thyme if you stand in the right place," Sam said. "City in front of us, pines behind us. We lived on one floor of a building my father had built with his own crews—a building where each level was a different family. Five kids. Doors that stayed open. Neighbors didn't need to be invited; living next door was invitation enough."

Adam listened, chin on the rail.

"You stood on the balcony, in a neighborhood of tightly knit buildings," Sam continued, "and you learned the patterns—habits, not just names. The aunt preparing six o'clock tea. The student hunched over his desk by lamplight. The boy dribbling a soccer ball in the stairwell until the echo became a heartbeat."

"You talk like the place is still there," Adam said.

"It will always live in my head," Sam replied. "And it's under all that water somewhere. Memory doesn't drown."

He unfolded his past like a map he hadn't dared open in years. The move from a lively working-class neighborhood that smelled of fresh bread and diesel to a small town nestled in the pines, where silence and birdsong stitched together three years of loneliness. Then another move—not to a lively neighborhood, not to a quiet pine town either, but to something in between, grocery shutters rattling at dawn, the butcher throwing bones to dogs at dusk. The school was close enough to walk to, the factories close enough to smell. A rotation of siblings at the table, pencils and elbows colliding. A mother performing small miracles with a pan. A father rubbing his eyebrows when the news was bad.

"There was war," he said softly, "but the mountains kept it at arm's length—a strange, shared denial. Once, we walked through three towns and back searching for a specific toy car in every shop we passed, and finding it felt like an adventure. And I drove my mother's car at fifteen—no one minded. In a war-torn country, the laws bent, and the town's slow, familiar streets felt like a village anyway—quiet, forgiving. And home... Home was always full. That was the measure: full."

He laughed at a memory. "And girls... I liked girls the way I liked oxygen. In high school, I was certain love was the compass of the universe. Mine pointed toward a girl whose building I could see from our balcony if I squinted. She would pass the grocer's at exactly four ten every afternoon. You can plan your life around a single minute without even realizing it."

Adam made a slight sound of recognition, no confession required.

"We weren't rich," Sam went on. "But we weren't poor. We were … woven. Our house was the loom. As my brothers left one by one—work, studies—I started making breakfast every morning just to keep us together ten minutes longer. When my turn came, I left for a university far away. I had stepped away from the very world that once held me steady."

"But you lived," Adam said.

"I lived," Sam agreed. "Flourished, even. America was generous. It gave me a new language, a new purpose, work, and possibilities. But at night, the room next door was empty—no brother playing music through the wall. No sister slamming a closet door. No aunt arguing with the TV. I looked out at new lights and didn't know whose lamp was whose."

A soft swell lifted the *Sea Glass*, then set it down gently.

"I found beauty there, too—mountains that stretched on for eternity, roads that felt like promises. But I never stopped missing the beauty back home. And when I visited—every year or two, if I could manage it—I'd keep the trip secret from my parents until the last minute, so they wouldn't wear holes in the floor waiting. I'd walk in, and for a heartbeat, nothing was said. Then everything all at once."

He paused, the waves slapping against the hull.

"Once," he said, "I went back to my old school, and the bell rang in the middle of the day. The same tone. The same rush— kids flooding the hall like water through a gate. Thirty years gone, and my legs still wanted to run with them. I used to sit under a column there, watching a girl I'd convinced myself was the axis of the universe. Silly, maybe. But the column remembered."

Adam smirked. "Dad, that's dramatic—but genuinely so."

"I hold degrees in both," Sam said, and they laughed.

He told Adam about movie nights—old Bruce Lee tapes, and a 007 film that once felt like a miracle and now looked like cardboard. "I showed it to your mother later; she looked at me like I'd brought her a knock-off carnival prize. But the theme song still turned the air gold."

A gull sliced across the sky, a precise stroke of white on blue.

"So… is that why this journey matters to you?" Adam asked gently.

Sam exhaled. "Because the flood erased the parts of the map that kept me oriented. I need to know what survived that isn't a grid line. Is the fig tree behind my parents' house still standing on the ridge? Are the people who knew my gait by sound still out there? Is the neighborhood still alive in the mountain town everyone escapes to in the summer?"

He turned to Adam, voice lower. "We say we're going east to check on family—and we are. But I'm also going to see if the school bell still rings, even if it hangs on a different wall."

The distance between them briefly collapsed.

"And," Sam added softly, "when you're pulled up by the roots, planting yourself again is the only cure I've found. Maybe not where you were; maybe just where the soil will take you. But you plant yourself. And you teach the next person how."

Adam watched a ripple on the water smooth into nothing. "I think I get it. When we were drifting after the storm, I thought about..." He hesitated. "I thought about someone."

Sam didn't turn. "You don't owe me her name."

"I don't have it," Adam lied, and Sam accepted that lie.

"It wasn't really about her," Adam said. "More about how people become your map. A place becomes a person, a person becomes a place. And if I ever get to say what I wanted to say to her, it'll mean I'm still me."

Sam nodded. "Yes. That."

Adam exhaled softly. "People and places get woven together inside you. Long for one, and you feel the pull of the other."

A long, smooth swell lifted them again, the convoy rising and falling in unison—a quiet choreography no one had rehearsed.

"I had a friend from India in college," Sam said. "He'd show me pictures of home and swear it was the most beautiful place on Earth. I didn't see it then, but I see it now. Beauty is an inside job. It lives in familiarity—in how your feet memorize streets, your tongue memorizes bakeries, your heart memorizes rituals. America taught me to admire the great wide open. But my home taught me to love the near."

"And this new world?" Adam asked, gesturing at the vast horizon.

"This new world asks us to make near out of far," Sam said. "To turn a convoy into a neighborhood. To turn sheriffs into uncles and radio clerks into the kid at the corner store. When we reach those mountains..." He nodded at a faint smudge that might have been clouds, land, or just wishful thinking. "… we'll see what's left of the old nearness, and bring what we can from the new."

They stood there gazing at the water long enough for a school of silver fish to stitch itself into a gleam and disappear. The radio clicked—a reminder that they were between windows—then went quiet again.

"Do you ever worry," Adam asked, "that when we get there, it'll feel wrong?"

"I worry," Sam said. "But I learned something backward. When I visited after moving away, everything looked shabby at first, until I sat at my mother's kitchen table. Then the paint peeled in the right places. The tea tasted right. The city hadn't changed—my heart just remembered how to see it."

He shrugged. "We won't get the whole thing back. Maybe a room. Maybe a corner. Maybe a bell on a different building. Maybe just a person who says, 'You're late,' and means, 'You're home.' That's enough."

A cloud ribboned across the sky. On the far side of the convoy, a diver surfaced and passed a sealed pouch to a nearby boat—the wave-rider postal service. Somewhere aft, someone idly strummed a guitar; the wind stole the melody and carried it away.

"You know," Adam said, "the sheriffs in New York said Mars hears our windows and answers with science and patience. If we're building a bridge there, and rebuilding one here, then the job is … staying long enough to finish."

Sam chuckled. "Human civilization: mechanical engineering and decency."

"And breakfast," Adam added.

"Which I can still make." Sam nudged him. "I used to push eggs at your uncles just to keep them in their chairs longer. The extra ten minutes were the whole point."

"You did that in Haven-3," Adam said. "When you kept the night-shift clerk talking, so he wouldn't sit alone and afraid."

"The plant leans toward the sun that first reached it," Sam said. "Even in a different pot."

The sun climbed, the waves turning from glass to silk. Evening drew the convoy closer. Radios flickered, alive with brief reports in a dozen languages. The familiar government cadence cut through at the window: *We stand with Earth. Report. Repair. Ration. Respond.* Ordinary words that had become holy.

"Ready to plant again?" Adam asked.

Sam looked east. Somewhere, mountains waited. Somewhere, if grace held, were parents, siblings, and cousins who still remembered his footsteps.

"Always," he said.

A shadow approached. Barlow had been listening.

"You boys talk like philosophers," he said. "Waves don't award degrees for that."

Adam grinned. "You've been quiet for once."

"Listening," Barlow said. "A sailor's trick. Wind talks more than waves, and people more than both. Since you've opened the book, I'll add a page."

His posture changed, like a cloud passing over the sun.

"I had a family once," he said. "Four kids. A wife who could out-sail me and out-curse me. We lived near the coast—high enough, we thought. Dogs that barked at the incoming tide like they were protecting the house from time itself."

He swallowed.

"When the storm came, her choice of weapon wasn't the wind. It was the sea pretending to be sky. I tried to reach them—tried until my last plank broke. Never found one of them."

The silence was heavy. Adam's hand curled around the rail; Sam stayed still.

"I didn't cry," Barlow said. "Couldn't. Like the world used up all my tears. So, I ride the waves now because they owe me an explanation. Every swell that rises, I tell it, 'Not today.' Every gale, I remind it who's still standing."

He let out a breath.

"I don't hate it. I just won't let it win again. The sea took what I had, so I made myself into something it couldn't take—a man too stubborn to sink."

He walked toward the helm, humming a melody like an off-key memory, and Sam and Adam finally understood the grief beneath his laughter.

***

Two days later, the calm betrayed them.

A Portuguese ship from the convoy hailed them by radio, its captain's voice steady, but edged with the kind of caution only the ocean could teach.

"Azores Carrier ahead on shared course," he said. *"Sheriffs are heavy near the Isles. Watch the southern reach."*

A pause.

"Bad water. Orcas."

He said it like a weather report, not a warning. In the post-storm world, predators had new routes, new behaviors. The ocean was a new curriculum, and everything in it—humans included—was a student.

Before the orcas appeared, the water went strangely glassy, as if the sea had stopped breathing to listen. A line of birds veered abruptly north. Even Barlow narrowed his eyes at the faintly wrong rhythm of the swells.

"They're out there," he murmured.

They saw the whales by midafternoon—black-and-white specters threading along the horizon, exhaling punctuation into the sky. At first, the sight was magnificent. Until it wasn't.

Barlow's mouth thinned. "They're not sightseeing."

The *Sea Glass* shuddered.

"Brace," he ordered. "They've learned to herd boats. Stay calm."

The first strike came without warning—a shoulder slam to the stern that snapped the world sideways. The vessel lifted into the air, showing the sky a flash of its belly before slamming back down.

138

The second hit rolled under the bow—deeper, deliberate, almost mocking.

Around them, the convoy tightened into instinctive formation, but the waves were already rewriting the rules.

"They're hunting," Barlow muttered. "Been watching us for days."

Chaos broke out in a rhythm that was too coordinated to be random. The whales moved like a unit, as though practicing a lesson humanity wished they'd never learned.

Barlow barked, "Noise!"

Someone unfurled a line bearing tin cans. They clattered and screeched across the surface.

The whales didn't care.

"Taste!" Barlow called.

They dumped engine coolant overboard. Toxic blue clouds mushroomed behind them. The pod hesitated, circling, evaluating.

Sam's heart hammered. He met Barlow's eyes. "It's not enough."

Barlow nodded grimly. "What, then?"

Sam hated the answer even as he said it. "Shock."

Barlow didn't argue. "Do it."

A crate marked SURVEY held sticks that weren't survey supplies at all—old fishing dynamite, a relic of another era. Sam wired a cap with trembling precision; Adam readied the throw line, knuckles white.

"On my mark," Barlow said. "Ahead of them, not at them. We're not soldiers. We're just loud."

Sam lit the fuse. The stick hissed. Adam hurled it far into the path of the next rising swell.

A heartbeat later, the ocean thumped—a deep, concussive *whumph* that collapsed the air in their lungs. Two shapes rolled onto their sides, stunned or dead, impossibly vast and heartbreakingly still. The rest of the pod veered off, their retreat carefully avoiding them.

Silence fell, jagged and uneasy. No one cheered.

Barlow rested a hand on the rail, gentle, as if touching a gravestone.

"We can't feed the waves with ourselves," he murmured. "Not today."

They sailed on in a bruised quiet.

By late afternoon, a shape rose out of the haze—a massive shadow resolving into hard edges and purposeful lines. The Azores Carrier emerged like a patient idea finally choosing to come to light. Cranes arched like arms. Flags snapped. Crew voices carried across the water, warm and alive.

Relief hit them like a forgotten feeling. They pulled up alongside by rope. Water by hose. Fuel by the drum. News by the boatload. Doctors on board stitched up wounds. Mechanics shared tools. Someone pressed warm food into Adam's hands before he could even ask. A shipboard guitarist strummed a tune that survived the wind this time.

Adam passed a salvaged coil of wire to a mechanic, who grinned. "You'll do," the man said.

As the sun lowered, Sam found Barlow alone at the bow, pipe clenched in his teeth, though it hadn't been lit in years. The man stared into the darkening water as if reading an old, half-forgotten ledger.

"You okay, Captain?" Sam asked.

Barlow exhaled a breath that might have been a laugh, or just fatigued.

"I've been worse," he said. "Waves tried again and failed. That's enough for today."

He turned, the wind flattening the gray in his beard. "You know, Doc," he said, voice softer, "every time I steer us out of something like that, I like to think that maybe—just maybe—my kids are somewhere laughing over their old man. Laughing because I'm still trying."

Sam didn't answer. Some silences are scripture.

Below them, the ocean breathed—vast and indifferent, the same relentless teacher it had always been. Above them, the smoke of the day drifted away into a fading sky. And between those two immensities, a single, stubborn boat kept heading east—toward a continent that might still remember their names. A faint scent of pine and salt threaded through the wind, like a distant memory leaning forward to say, *"Keep going."*

New Europe

For days, the horizon had been nothing but a vague promise—long, wavering lines of haze that seemed to fold the world inward. The convoy held course east, sun-bleached and salt-spattered, engines humming in uneasy unison. They'd been at sea long enough that the groaning of the hull had worked itself into their heartbeats— even its tired creaks had started to sound like complaints. The maps were old, the currents had changed, and the birds seemed lost. Europe lay ahead in stories only.

Captain Barlow stood at the helm of the *Sea Glass*, squinting at the distant blur of dawn as if he could will the continent back into definition. His beard had gone feral in the wind, his voice raspy from salt and stubbornness.

"Europe," he said, leaning forward, "used to mean trains, museums, cathedrals, coffee that costs too damn much. Now? She's got more wounds than wonders."

Sam leaned beside him on the rail. "Have you heard any rumors?"

"Plenty." Barlow spat into the froth below. "Never had time to unify before the flood. Too many flags, too many debts. When the water came, everyone fought for whatever wasn't drowning. Some kept navies. Others kept guns. The rest kept grudges."

Thirty vessels stretched behind them—a ragged line of patched hulls, reborn sailboats, jury-rigged skimmers, and converted trawlers in a little flotilla stitched together by need, nerve, and a sliver of American stubbornness. Radio calls patrolled the convoy like ghostly sheriffs: *"Maintain formation ... rations check ... report contact."*

By dusk, Sam and Adam sat on the aft deck, watching the western sky bruise purple above the swells.

Adam tapped the edge of a solar panel crusted with salt. "He makes it sound like we're sailing into hell."

Barlow's laugh rolled from the bridge. "Hell's just land with old scars, boy! Keep your head, and hell minds its manners."

That night, the radio flickered with ghost frequencies—broken broadcasts in half a dozen languages, fading in and out like dreams. Clipped commands, cracked hymns, laughter warped by static— civilization reflected in broken mirrors.

A woman from another ship joined them at the mess hall and leaned forward with a conspiratorial whisper.

"A French pilot says half the continent is afloat now," she said. "Towns built on platforms and tethered ships. They call them flotillas. The rest are 'keeps'—mountain fortresses rebuilt into cities."

"Fortresses?" Sam echoed.

"They trade by air and convoy. "Everything below the mountain keeps..." Her voice trailed off. "That's pirate territory."

Barlow grunted. "Always someone ready to steal instead of build."

"And the Vatican?" someone asked.

"Oh, it floats," she said, eyes bright with awe. "A sacred island. People die trying to reach it."

Sam pictured marble domes adrift on black water—a strange mix of hope and ghostliness.

"And we're sailing into this?" he murmured.

Barlow shrugged. "Roots are roots. Yours run east. Mine run wherever there's a fight worth winning."

***

Morning came yellow and metallic—the kind of light that weighs on the eyes, and the kind of air that leaves a taste on the tongue. Sam was sketching a repair plan for the bilge pump when something flickered across the water—thin, silver, fast. Then another. Then an entire swarm.

"South approach! Fast craft!"yelled a lookout. "South approach! Fast craft!"

The water erupted with speedboats—stitched-together nightmares built from Jet Skis, scrap aluminum, plastic drums, and anything that could take an engine. Figures crouched on decks, armor pieced together from motorcycle gear and welded steel. Masks glared with painted teeth. Flags snapped in the wind—skulls, inverted tricolors, broken anchors, symbols born of anarchy and desperation.

Barlow was already moving. "Convoy break pattern! Scatter into groups of three! You can't circle what you can't count!"

Engines roared. The convoy split apart like startled birds. The raiders howled as they closed in—raw, animal, gleefully violent.

The first grappling hook clanged against the *Sea Glass's* rail. Adam swung an oar, dislodging it. A hand reached up from below, fingers wrapped in tape and glinting with rings. Sam grabbed a wrench and slammed downward. The hand vanished with a hiss of pain.

Gunfire cracked from a nearby ship. The air was filled with burning fuel and salt. The stench of fear spread like smoke.

Barlow shouted through the storm, "Brace port side—ram incoming!"

A raider boat skimmed parallel to their vessel. One of its crew leapt onto the deck, chain whipping through the air. Sam ducked as metal sliced the space where his head had been. They collided, slamming into the rail. The raider snarled behind a tin mask with iron fangs. Sam's wrench met bone and metal. The man toppled backward into the churning waves.

Another raider clambered over the bow; Adam fired a warning shot into the air. The sound cracked like thunder.

"Do not waste ammunition!" Barlow roared. "Only shoot what you aim to bury!"

The *Sea Glass* lurched as a skimmer slammed into the stern. Adam was thrown forward, rolled, and rose bleeding from the temple.

Barlow's eyes flashed. "Keep breathing! That's all victory ever asks!"

Lightning forked overhead. The ocean lit up white and black. The convoy was scattered across miles now—some burning, some fleeing, some fighting alone. Sam glimpsed a ship exploding on the horizon—a bloom of orange that swallowed its silhouette and scattered debris.

"Dad!" Adam yelled. "Starboard flank!"

Three skimmers bore down on them. One raider hurled a Molotov cocktail; it hit the water just short of the boat, flames erupting across the waves like molten blooms.

Barlow slammed the throttle. The *Sea Glass* leapt forward like an untethered beast, its wake like a sea wall, smashing the nearest raider into capsizing. Two more swerved, one losing control and slamming into the burning wreckage.

"That's right!" Barlow howled. "Learn the waves, or drown in 'em!"

But for every raider that fell, two more surged forward. They regrouped with unsettling discipline—circling, probing, attacking in coordinated arcs.

"They're starving," Barlow growled. "Hunger forces strategy."

The storm worsened. Waves climbed up into walls. The *Sea Glass* groaned with each crest. Sam's knuckles bled from the pump handle. Salt cake coated every rope.

To port, a ship cried out for help, its captain screaming coordinates. A red flare rose, then a white one.

Barlow's jaw clenched. "We can't break formation again. They'll take us down one by one."

"What do we do?" Sam asked.

"We endure," Barlow said. "And we wait for Europe to remember she still has teeth."

147

The sun dropped behind a curtain of bruised clouds. Firelight dotted the swells—burning hulls, flaming oil slicks, smoldering debris. The raiders tightened behind the convoy like wolves circling a herd of wounded deer.

Barlow watched them with a sailor's fatalistic calm.

"They think they're closing the trap," he muttered. "They don't know that Europe's got nightmares of her own."

At that moment, the world exploded in white.

Search beams tore through the haze—massive, blinding. Rotary gunfire thundered. Turbine engines shrieked across the water.

Through the smoke emerged forms of war—three towering ships, hulls armored, weapon pods bristling, decks lined with gunners. Their national colors were faded, but surviving: France. Italy. Spain.

The Western Alliance.

Tracer fire illuminated the waves. Raiders split up and fled. Explosions lit up the storm like a false dawn.

Barlow threw his head back and laughed—a laugh of disbelief and delirious joy.

"There she is!" he roared. "Civilization remembering how to roar!"

Within minutes, the raiders were shattered. Within half an hour, silence had replaced the storm.

A voice crackled through the radio—female, crisp, heavily accented.

"Convoy Seventeen, you are under Alliance protection. Maintain heading zero-eight-four. Medical teams ready."

Barlow sagged against the wheel, exhausted and triumphant. "Told you, boys. Europe might be bleeding, but she ain't dead."

***

By dawn, the water was a graveyard of wreckage. Only twelve ships remained out of thirty. The Alliance destroyers shepherded them east, guiding them through a broken metal corridor of floating checkpoints: drone platforms humming with surveillance, old oil rigs retrofitted into watchtowers, pontoons draped with the stitched-together European triad flag.

Barlow stood at the bow, arm wrapped in rough gauze. The bandage had darkened overnight, but he ignored it.

Ahead, mountains rose from the sea, gray spines cutting into the sky—the Alps. What once held ski lodges and serene villages now supported solar arrays, wind vanes, rope trams, and moored airships swaying like tethered birds. Terraces cut into the rock glowed with the light of hydroponic farms. Smoke curled from the chimneys—real wood smoke.

"Welcome to the keeps," the radio announced. *"Proceed to Dock Seven for inspection. Law is in effect."*

"Law?" Barlow scoffed. "Up here, altitude is law."

The *Sea Glass* moored alongside other survivors, greeted by guards in mismatched uniforms. They inspected cargo, confiscated makeshift weapons, and scanned layers of quarantine protocols.

149

"You'll get two days' rest," a clerk told them. "Then assignments. This refuge works, not shelters."

Barlow smiled thinly. "Ma'am, rest sounds too good to be true."

Sam took in the drowned world below—old valleys submerged beneath shimmering mirrors, rooftops scattered like floating fossils.

"They've turned mountains into islands," he murmured.

"The world turned itself," Barlow replied. "We just had to learn to see it with fresh eyes."

At night, the new arrivals gathered in a hall built from salvaged timber. A young officer pointed to holographic maps displaying Europe's fractured state.

"The Western Alliance controls the mountains and mid-altitudes," she said. "The coastal zones are lawless—pirates in the sea, militias along the ridges. The Vatican floats west of Rome—still sovereign. No-fly zones over Old Vienna. The Balkan territories are contested."

Sam scribbled notes in his journal. The scholar in him awakened, trying to catalog chaos.

Barlow leaned back, smirking. "Same song, new verse."

After the meeting, snow began to fall—a gentle, swirling drift. Adam caught flakes on his palm, eyes wide.

"Snow," he exhaled. "Real snow."

Barlow watched him, a strange paternal shadow crossing his expression. "Don't get too comfortable, lad. Peace in these parts melts even faster than that."

***

By morning, Barlow's bandaged arm had swollen beneath the linen, angry red streaks running up toward his shoulder. He hid it as long as he could, adjusting ropes one-handed, barking orders with his usual force—but Sam saw the stiffness in his movements, the dull wince each time he braced against the ship's rail.

Sam found him in the galley, gripping a bolt with his good hand, trying and failing to tighten it.

"You should see the medic," Sam said.

"Medic's for the soft," Barlow muttered, though his voice had lost its usual gravel. He paused, leaning on the counter for balance. "Besides ... I've had worse."

"Not this kind," Sam answered quietly.

Barlow shot him a half-hearted scowl, but his knees wobbled. Pride had always been the thickest armor he wore—tougher than leather, heavier than steel. But even pride had seams.

Sam and Adam walked him to the mountain infirmary—formerly a monastery, now a place of antiseptic and urgent murmurs. Stone arches. Cold light. The air smelled of iodine and something older, like abandoned prayers.

A nurse approached, eyes assessing Barlow before she spoke.

"You waited too long," she said, not unkindly. "Maybe not too long to save something … but certainly too long for comfort."

She began cleansing the wound. Barlow clenched his jaw, but didn't make a sound. When she stepped away to prepare poultices, Barlow turned to Sam and Adam with the faintest flash of humor.

"Don't look at me like that. The sea's treated me worse, and I'm still here."

Adam swallowed. "We need you here."

Barlow smirked. "Boy, needing a man never stopped the sea from taking him."

The fever rose by afternoon. His skin flushed hot; his eyes shimmered with the glaze of a drifting mind. They moved him to a quiet stone chamber at the far end of the infirmary, where wind seeped through cracks in the old mortar and candlelight flickered uneasily.

Sam sat with him, notebook open, sensing without knowing why that what Barlow said now mattered more than anything he'd said before.

"It was the third day of the storm," Barlow whispered, voice drifting like a tide pulling away. "The roof went. The fence went. The whole damn world went."

His eyes closed, but his mind stayed open.

"Wife kept shouting at the wind. Said she wouldn't let God push her around. Kids in the cellar with the dogs, laughing. *Laughing*, Doc. As if it were a game."

He paused, breath rattling.

"I pulled the youngest out the window. The boy said it felt like camping. Then a branch scraped the hull—just a branch, but carrying half a tree. Hit us broadside."

He swallowed thickly.

"Next thing I remember, I'm clutching driftwood. Woke up to silence that never ended. Never found them. House gone. Land gone. World gone."

The room didn't move, but something inside Sam did.

"What did you do?" he asked softly.

"What every fool does after he loses everything." Barlow smiled faintly. "I built something out of the ruins. Built myself a boat. Said if I couldn't save mine, I'd save someone else's. Guess I've been doing that ever since."

His voice faded into a murmur.

"But I ain't cried once. Should've. Wanted to. Guess the sea took the salt outta me."

Sam closed his notebook slowly. "You've saved people," he said quietly. "You saved us."

Barlow let out a weak chuckle. "Don't thank me yet. Still breathing—that's the easy part."

Evening fell fast—the kind of blue twilight that feels fragile. Then came the alarm.

A deep, metallic bellow shook the rocks. Boots thundered overhead. Someone shouted, "Raiders on the lower lake!"

Sam and Adam rushed outside. The lake below shimmered black beneath the cliffs, its surface breaking into silver lines—wakes, approaching too quickly.

It was the raiders—the ones who'd survived—following the convoy's trail.

The fortress transformed instantly—soldiers sprinting to elevated posts, farmers grabbing tools forged into weapons, children ushered inside by adults with steeled faces. Searchlights illuminated. Guns took aim. The mountain held its breath.

Barlow appeared at the parapet, arm bound tight, eyes feverish but fierce.

"You shouldn't be up here," Sam said.

Barlow ignored him, shouldering a rifle with his good arm. "Not sitting this one out. Been fighting pirates since before you were changing diapers."

No one argued. You don't tell the storm to rest.

Boats appeared—dark shapes slicing toward the base of the cliffs. Gunfire cracked. Echoes bounced between the peaks like trapped thunder.

A hook snagged the lower wall. Sam and Adam leaned over, hauling the line upward, hacking it free. Defenders above poured down burning oil. Flames streaked the lake orange. Screams rose, then were swallowed by the water.

Barlow fired steadily, controlled, unshakeable, even as his feverish hand trembled.

Another boat sank. Another fled. Smoke crawled across the waves.

Only when the last raider drifted into silence did Barlow's strength falter. He sagged against the wall, breath wheezing.

"Reckon…" he muttered, "… I'm running low on fuel."

They carried him back inside. He was burning up. The nurse took one look at him and tightened her jaw.

"Rest now," she said softly, her hand on the door. "All of you."

Her voice held no judgment, no finality—just inevitability.

"We'll do what we can," she added. "But … you must let life take its course."

There was a strange softness in the way she closed the door behind them, almost like someone shielding a candle from the wind.

Later that night, the wind howled down the valley like the sea remembering itself. Barlow lay propped up in his bunk, breath shallow but steady, a small wooden chest beside him, the varnish worn off by a lifetime of hands.

He nudged it toward Sam.

"Family's things. Photos. Trinkets. Compass. Nonsense to most folk. But gold to me. Can't take it where I'm going."

Sam opened his mouth, but Barlow raised a trembling hand.

"If any of mine ever find you … anyone with a face like mine or a question on their tongue … give them this. Tell 'em I went down fighting. Not flinching."

Adam swallowed hard. "You're not going anywhere."

Barlow smiled—not weak, not fading, but knowing.

"Son ... the tide's halfway out already. But it's a good tide. Gentler than most."

He rested his hand atop Sam's.

"You build your life out of calm, if you can. The world's got enough storms."

His eyes drifted half-closed.

"Good lads ... both of you..."

His breathing evened—slow, rhythmic, distant, like waves pulling back from the shore.

Sam and Adam sat with him long after the candles burned low.

At some point, Sam realized the rhythm in the room had changed—not breaking, just slipping into something quieter—a gentler pattern, thinner, like a memory of breath rather than breath itself.

He didn't call the nurse. He didn't move. He let the moment be what it was.

***

When dawn crawled pale across the mountains, the bed was empty. Not disturbed. Not in chaos. Just empty.

A blanket was folded. The wooden chest sat where Sam had placed it. The room was colder than it had been the night before.

The nurse met them at the doorway—a woman whose face had seen too many endings to fear them anymore. Her voice was steady.

"There comes a time," she said, "when we let go … and let life carry someone where they need to go next."

The mountain air held its silence with the reverence of a book closed.

Sam carried the chest back to the *Sea Glass*, Adam walking beside him. Neither spoke. The town around them was already waking—repairing walls, heating water, tallying ammunition. Life moved on, stubborn as roots cracking stone.

At the dock, the Alliance clerk approached with a tablet.

"Convoy forming south," she said. "Bound for the Levant. Small but disciplined. You're cleared to join if you can work."

Sam nodded. "We can."

She glanced at the wooden chest. "Personal effects?"

Sam shook his head. "History. A friend's."

She didn't pry further.

***

They pushed off under a sky that smelled of thawed snow and diesel. The mountains shrank behind them, peaks like old sentinels watching them go.

Sam secured the chest in his cabin, wrapping it in cloth to keep the salt away. Adam joined him on deck, his face a little older than it had been yesterday.

"Feels wrong to leave him," Adam said.

Sam looked out over the silver water. "It would've felt wrong to stay. He knew that."

They stood together at the rail. The sea deepened to steel blue. The radio crackled with the cadence of the new convoy—fewer voices, calmer ones. Hope in a different rhythm.

Adam pointed toward the horizon, where the sun glinted off the water like scattered coins. "That way?"

Sam followed his gaze. "That way. Toward whatever's left … and what's still possible."

He rested his hand on the rail, whispering a wordless prayer for Eisha and Sarah somewhere across the waves. For the friend whose absence was a presence. For the world that refused to die quietly.

The engines rumbled to life. The convoy angled southeast, chasing the sun. Behind them, the mountains faded—not as a loss, but as a witness. The faint scent of pine drifted across the water one last time, a reminder that some things, even drowned, still rise. And perhaps some things thought long gone are only waiting to be found again.

Heading East

The docks were louder now—engines, barter, laughter, and rumor all clattering together against the iron spine of the new Europe—its ports, rails, and anchored hulls. In this world, convoys didn't have governments; they had momentum. And momentum ruled more effectively than any parliament ever had.

This morning, the air smelled like diesel, salt, woodsmoke, and hope. People of every tongue and heritage crowded the piers, swapping stories, negotiating for passage, tying knots that might decide their survival. Fleets were built the way hives once were—through shared need, borrowed faith, and a desperation that welded strangers into temporary families.

Sam and Adam moved through the noise with their bags slung over their shoulders, following the long pier stretching like a gangplank into an uncertain future. Behind them, the last of the European highlands jutted from the water, jagged ruins of old nations now swallowed by the sea. Ships of every size pressed against one another, patched hulls bearing welded fragments of cities that no longer existed. Hand-painted flags fluttered—sunbursts, crests, old emblems distorted into new meanings. A man with a bullhorn shouted, "Middle East convoy forming! East route through Anatolia and beyond—Lebanon, Cyprus, maybe farther!"

Those last two words—"maybe farther"—held more gravity than any official map. *Maybe farther* meant there were still blank spaces in the world.

Around them, conversations flowed like currency. Each captain preached their own gospel about the world beyond the horizon.

A Spanish woman with arms like mooring lines lifted her coffee. "Crete's safe if you cling to the cliffs. Inland gangs?" She snorted. "Still feeding on their own stories."

A lean man with a silver tooth spoke without looking up. "New towns in the Aegean. Built on mountaintops, where goats graze on roofs. The future's vertical."

And then came Captain Darwish.

He stepped through the crowd like a rumor in black boots. His jaw looked carved from a broken anchor, his posture that of a man who'd bargained with storms, and his voice sounded brewed from bitter coffee and diesel.

He drew a crude map on the lid of a crate, marking the lines with thick charcoal.

"Turkey's still got ports above water," he said. "Trade's alive. But so are the factions. Rogues. Old coast guard militias. They fight over what they can't build. And every one of them believes the sea belongs to their dead grandparents."

Adam leaned closer. "And Lebanon?"

Darwish's smile deepened into something equal parts fondness and warning. "High mountains, high pride. The coast's mostly gone. But the mountains live. Some people float in cities. Others drift on grudges." He shrugged. "The water there holds more stories than fish."

A gust carried the scent of brine, engine oil, and toasted flatbread. Around them, crews loaded water barrels, solar stills, fishing lines, old batteries, and crates of preserved food. A woman spun in circles, handing bread to strangers, laughing as if the world had not drowned. Everyone understood: convoys survived because people remembered how to share.

By evening, Sam had signed their names into Darwish's battered leather log, older than some of the ships. Their assigned vessel, *Hera's Wake*, was built from the bones of three boats welded together like mismatched ribs. It smelled of tar and garlic. Its gun mounts gleamed with fresh oil. Its crew was a patchwork of accents, old loyalties, and stitched-up scars.

Darwish looked at Sam and Adam with something between welcome and warning. "We sail at dawn. Pray to whatever gods you still believe in. The sea has its own—and she's moody."

***

Hera's Wake left port beneath a clean dawn and a dirty flag. Seventeen ships followed: fishing trawlers reborn as miniature freighters, old ferries turned lifeboat carriers, even a quasi-submarine that glided like a half-whispered rumor.

For the first week, the waves behaved. The air softened. Radios chimed like migrating birds. Songs drifted across frequencies—old ballads, half-forgotten anthems, new rhythms born of collapse and perseverance.

Adam and Sam spent evenings against the railing, watching the convoy stretch and contract with the tide. Some nights, it felt like a floating city—other nights, like seventeen fragile hopes held together by fraying rope.

On the ninth morning, the wind changed.

At first, it was subtle—small taps against the hull, the sea testing its teeth. The crew noticed before Sam or Adam. Darwish muttered something in Arabic, a prayer sailors used when instinct tightened the chest.

Then came the echoes. Sharp. Rhythmic. Too deliberate for thunder.

A burst of static ripped through the radio. Voices shouted coordinates. Orders snapped through clipped signals. Sam and Adam scrambled to the topside.

Across the horizon, fast boats appeared—sleek silhouettes cutting through the water with purpose. They moved in coordinated formations, not like pirates, but like militias— remnants of old coastal conflicts. Some bore faded national crests. Others displayed clenched fists, suns, or stylized waves. Their hulls were armored with welded plates, scavenged steel, and pieces of wreckage.

Tracer rounds carved bright lines across the water.

"Engines full!" Darwish roared.

Hera's Wake lurched forward, engines howling. Gun crews snapped into place with frightening efficiency.

A crack split the air as a round ricocheted off the railing near Adam, spraying steel splinters.

"Dad—what do they want?!" Adam shouted.

162

"Territory. Supplies. An excuse," Sam said.

"Trespassing? On water?"

Sam gave a grim shrug. "After the flood, everyone drew lines they can't see."

The first militia boat veered close. Men shouted in Turkish and Arabic. A chain launcher fired, its hook clanging against *Hera's Wake's* bow. The crew severed the chain instantly.

A second boat flanked them. The gunner fired controlled bursts—precise, minimal, deadly. Water plumed around the craft, forcing it to retreat.

A third came in low and fast. A masked man leapt for the railing—but Adam reacted on instinct, swinging an oar from a storage rack. The blow struck the man's chest cleanly. He tumbled backward into the frothing wake.

Another climber made it halfway up the hull before a bullet found him. He fell without a sound.

Darwish swung the wheel sharply, sending *Hera's Wake* cutting across a wave ridge. The convoy scattered, each ship breaking formation to evade pursuit.

Minutes stretched like a taut rope. Gunfire echoed. Smoke rose from two militia vessels. A third was ripped apart after a direct hit.

Eventually, the remaining attackers fled eastward in broken arcs. Silence returned in slow, uneven breaths. The waves heaved on, oblivious to the burst of violence.

On deck, a medic worked over a wounded crewman—shrapnel in his leg. He winced, then laughed at his own pain.

"You'll have a limp," the medic said. "But you'll live. In this world, that's a promotion."

Darwish wiped blood from his cheek. "Sometimes they're friendly," he told Adam. "Today was one of their polite days."

Adam's pulse was still racing. "People do this every day?"

"In the new world?" Darwish shrugged. "Some people don't have days—they only have fights."

Gradually, the ship resumed its rhythm. Crews patched hulls, inventoried lost gear, and shared bitter jokes. Someone brewed coffee on a burner, the smell drifting through the air like living proof that civilization hadn't entirely drowned.

Sam sat with Adam at the bow, both staring eastward.

"Every attack," Sam said, "reminds you how precious every calm day is."

Darwish nodded. "The farther east you go, the fewer calm days you get. But the sweet ones? They taste even sweeter."

***

Turkey appeared the next morning—what little remained of it. It rose from the water like a broken necklace, peaks and ridges jutting from the sea, the highest mountaintops now islands. Terrestrial life clung stubbornly to stone—terraced farms, suspended solar panels, makeshift cables strung between cliffs.

They navigated between spines of rock and floating docks anchored by chains as thick as saplings. The port was called Yeni

Kaya—"New Rock," a cluster of platforms suspended between two surviving peaks. Men in patched uniforms guided them with hand signals. Rifles hung at their sides—reminders, not threats. Turkey had learned caution.

A market sprawled across floating barges and cliffside stalls. Vendors sold dried fruit, preserved meats, coils of wire, and ammunition cartridges. Children carried buckets of desalinated water and traded them for bread. Teenagers hauled crates of lemons from mountaintop orchards.

A loudspeaker repeated a warning in three languages: *"Stay near the docks. The mountains are not kind."*

Darwish led them into a café carved into the rock itself. Lanterns glowed warmly. The coffee could have woken a ghost.

"They say the inland is dangerous," Adam murmured.

"Danger is just need with bad manners," Darwish replied. "People up there lost everything. They take from whoever wanders." He sipped. "Stay on your boat, you're a guest. Step inland, you're the loot."

Adam blinked. "The loot?"

Darwish smirked. "Let's just say you don't want to find out."

Outside, Sam watched a line of men haul crates up a switchback trail. Higher still, the skeletal remains of an old highway curled through rubble—a fossil of civilization.

They stayed only a few hours. By evening, the convoy's engines rumbled anew. *Hera's Wake* turned south, following the Anatolian ridge.

Darwish stood at the bow, wind catching his hair. "Tomorrow," he said quietly, "you'll see Lebanon. Maybe your past will be staring back at you."

Sam's chest tightened. "You think it'll still look like home?"

Darwish's eyes softened. "Home," he said, "is the one place that hurts right."

***

For twelve days, the convoy drifted through brightening seas. The water shifted from slate to turquoise. Breezes warmed. Tension loosened. On the twelfth dawn, morning arrived as though the world had suddenly remembered beauty.

A shout rang out from the bridge—

"There! Mountains ahead!"

Through thinning mist, the world unfolded.

Lebanon. A spine of evergreen and stone rising directly from the sea, peaks catching the sunlight like polished silver. Terraces clung to the slopes—some ancient, some improvised, all stubborn. Solar-paneled roofs winked between the cedars, wind turbines spinning high above. Fishing boats dotted the water like scattered confetti.

Sam stood at the bow, chest tightening with something he hadn't felt since before the flood. Nostalgia. Longing. Fear of being forgotten.

Darwish joined him. "You're looking at one of the few places that held onto its beauty." He gestured toward the ridges—enduring, stubborn, sacred. "Did you know that Lebanon is mentioned in the Old Testament more than seventy times?" he said quietly. "A land of cedars and promise. Moses begged God to let him cross the Jordan and see 'that goodly mountain, and Lebanon.'" He paused. "And God answered, 'Enough. Speak no more of this.'"

The mountains shimmered like memory. Sam swallowed, feeling a longing so fierce that even Scripture couldn't soothe it. Here he was, returning to a land of both blessings and ache.

As they drew nearer, the water thickened with life. Fishermen shouted greetings in Arabic, nets heavy with silver fish. Children waved from the floating markets. Laughter drifted on the wind.

"It's alive," Adam whispered.

"Lebanon always was," Sam replied.

Then the world cracked open.

A sudden burst of gunfire erupted from the south—sharp, frantic, unmistakable. Two flotillas were trading rounds across the water, rafts stacked with barrels and patched canopies bobbing in chaos. Flags with faded icons whipped violently. Men shouted over the crash of waves and weapons.

Darwish swore. "Hold tight! We cut through now, or we get dragged into their morning argument."

Hera's Wake surged forward.

The two flotillas weren't shooting at the convoy—more a habit of disagreeing loudly. Stray rounds skipped across the water like malicious stones.

A flare screeched into the air, exploding in a shower of sparks over a raft. Smoke rose from another vessel listing sharply.

Adam ducked as a round struck the stern behind him. "They don't even see us!"

"They don't see anyone," Darwish growled. "Welcome to the Levant—they fight at dawn, trade by noon, dance by night."

Hera's Wake weaved between drifting debris and shrieking voices. Sam steadied Adam as the deck pitched beneath them. For five breathless minutes, it felt as though the world had shrunk to two objectives: don't get hit, and don't slow down.

Then, finally, the noise thinned. The smoke dispersed. The flotillas shrank into a distant quarrel. Silence rolled in like an exhausted tide.

Sam let out a long breath. "How do people live like this?"

Darwish didn't look back. "Same way they always have—with stubborn hearts and selective hearing."

They entered the harbor just north of what had once been Byblos. Water lapped against platforms lashed together like a giant spiderweb. Families sold fruit, nets, spices, hand-built tech— whatever the mountains could provide. A painted sign in Arabic, French, and English swung gently:

WELCOME TO JABAL AL NOUR – MOUNTAIN OF LIGHT

Darwish stopped at the main pier, gripping Sam's forearm.

"This is where I leave you. I'm heading south. Toward the Three Jerusalems."

Sam frowned. "Three?"

Darwish only smiled. "A story for another voyage." He handed Sam a sealed tin box. "Few coins, for luck. And if luck fails—for trade."

Sam clasped his hand. "Thank you. For everything."

Darwish made his way back to *Hera's Wake*, already shouting orders, as if sentimentality were something he'd traded away long ago.

The pier shuddered as Sam and Adam stepped onto solid ground. For weeks, the world had been nothing but water. Now the land rose steeply behind the harbor—crooked buildings leaning into cliffs, switchback roads curling like old scars, terraces clinging stubbornly to slopes. The air tasted different. Less salt. More earth. More history. Somewhere, a dog barked. It was such an ordinary sound that it almost broke Sam.

"We're really here," Adam breathed, almost in disbelief.

Sam nodded, unable to speak for a moment.

Officials scanned names and scribbled notes when their tablets died. A young officer kept glancing at Sam's manifest.

"Saphire," she said at last. "The ... anomaly scientist?"

Sam almost laughed. "That's what they called me."

Her expression softened. "My family listened to your broadcasts. We left the city because of you. Moved up into the hills. We're still there."

"I'm glad," Sam said—and meant it.

After hours of checks, a battered truck waited at the gate—a long-bed pickup with mismatched panels and a grill held together with rope. The driver leaned against the hood, holding a handmade sign: INLAND TRAVEL – SANNINE / ZAHLE / SHOUF / JEZZINE.

The man's name was Rami. Sam negotiated their passage quietly.

"We can trust him?" Adam whispered.

A nearby traveler answered for him. "They only allow trusted drivers in here. Speak less. Listen more."

Rami loaded their bags. "Ready?"

Sam looked back at the sea one last time—the boat was already refueling for another uncertain journey.

"We're ready."

The road climbed fast, hugging cliffs carved by landslides and time. The truck rattled. The view swung between the sky and the churning water far below. Adam pressed a hand to the window.

"It feels wrong," he said. "To move and not be on water."

Sam nodded. After weeks at sea, land felt too still—like the world had stopped breathing.

"Your legs will remember," Sam said.

But he wasn't sure if his heart would.

As the sun dimmed, Rami turned off the main road. More bends. Encroaching darkness. Bushes clawed at the sides of the truck.

"We'll kill the lights soon," Rami said.

"Why?" Adam asked.

Rami's jaw tightened. "Because some people decided the flood was their chance to start over as kings."

A moment later, he flicked the headlights off.

Darkness swallowed the world. Only starlight and the faint outline of a guardrail hinted at a road at all.

"Relax," Rami murmured. "If I go slow enough, the truck remembers the way."

The engine hummed low. Gravel crunched under the tires. Sam could feel the landscape through the vibration, feeling blind trust in a driver who had done this too many times to count.

"Why turn off the lights?" Adam asked uneasily.

"Because gangs watch from the ridges," Rami said. "They see a glow, they follow it. Land pirates. Same as at sea. We don't stop unless we must. If something blocks the road, we back up. No talking. No arguing. Understand?"

Adam nodded tightly.

For the next hour, the world narrowed to three things as the truck inched up the mountain road: the crawl of the truck, the scrape of branches on metal, and the shared breath of three men who knew some dangers were quieter than gunfire.

By dawn, lights began to appear ahead—warm, steady, safe. Small houses clung to a plateau like a community that had learned survival by clustering close. Sam felt something shift inside him, recognition blooming like an ache. They were close—very close.

Adam poked him gently. "Are we there yet?"

Sam laughed, almost cried.

What had once been a modest mountain village was now a thriving sanctuary. Homes clung to the hillside, stacked like lanterns. Solar panels shimmered in tiers. Terraces overflowed with strawberries, beans, mint, and thyme. Children chased one another around a fountain in the square.

And then—

"Sam?"

A voice behind them. Old. Familiar. Trembling.

Sam turned.

His brother stood frozen—older, grayer, but unmistakable.

"Ya Allah," he whispered. "It's him. It's Sam!"

Within seconds, the whole square erupted. Hands grabbed Sam's shoulders, his face, his arms, touching him to confirm that he wasn't a ghost. Tears. Laughter. Shouts. A whirlwind of familiarity.

His parents emerged slowly from a stone house at the square's edge. His father stopped mid-step. His mother's hands flew to her mouth.

"You're late," his father said, voice cracking—an old family joke.

Sam's reply came out broken. "I got lost."

Then they embraced—deep, fierce, dissolving years of distance and fear. Adam watched, tears slipping out quietly, until his grandmother seized him with the fierce tenderness only the Lebanese could wield.

"Teta," Adam breathed, using the word he loved for grandmother without thinking.

"You've grown!" she said, half laughing, half crying. "The world drowned, and you still grew. Good. That's what children do—grow, no matter what nonsense adults are making."

Inside, the house smelled of thyme, coffee, and the faint medicinal scent of eldercare. A hospital bed had been set in one corner, surrounded by photos from drier years—weddings, graduations, Sam holding a baby who was now taller than he'd ever imagined. Lentils simmered on the stove. A bowl of cut cucumbers and tomatoes sat forgotten beside a knife. Life had not stopped, only paused.

People flowed through—cousins, neighbors, old classmates—each repeating the same refrain:

"We thought you were gone!"

"We saw the storms."

"We prayed you'd found high ground."

At first, Sam let himself float in that tide of love. But gradually, the space at the bedside grew louder. His father was weakening.

***

Sam's father's final days bore a quiet, sacred gravity. Sam sat beside him one afternoon, light spilling through the window in thin gold streamers.

"I thought I said my goodbyes last time you visited," his father whispered. "Every time you leave, I wonder … is that the last time I will see your face?"

He looked at the ceiling, eyes shining. "When the storms came, I told God, 'If this is how it ends, fine. You made us. You can unmake us.' But I asked Him for one more thing—that I wouldn't die imagining you underwater." He chuckled softly. "He overdelivered. I got you both back. I even got to yell at you for not calling. That's more mercy than I deserve."

Sam's throat tightened. *"Baba…"*

"How else should I speak?" his father said gently. "I am old. My heart was made for dry land, and now the world is a sea. But it's happy, because you walked through my door one more time."

He reached for Adam's hand with surprising strength. "And you," he said. "You will carry the stories."

Adam swallowed hard.

His grandfather passed away three days later, in a silence so soft, it felt like the world holding its breath. Sam sat with him when the last exhale came—slow, steady, then no more.

Grief struck sharply—but beneath it was gratitude. Sam had said hello one more time, and goodbye almost in the same breath.

***

The funeral was small, but full of love—neighbors, family, old friends from the valley. Afterward, the house felt different—emptier, yet somehow fuller. Sam stayed by his mother, helping where he could. He studied the faces of his siblings, cousins, and the townsfolk. He felt the weight of survival, but also its blessings.

One night, Adam found him on the flat roof, staring at the hills.

"You okay?" he asked.

"No," Sam said. Then, after a pause, "But also yes. Maybe that's the only way it works now."

They sat together under sharp mountain stars. The world was broken, but this place—this roof, this valley—held its own kind of peace.

***

On the third day after the funeral, Adam met her.

The supply office was a renovated stone house, humming with screens and paper maps. Sam was inside finalizing route papers. Adam wandered…

… and stopped.

She stood near a window, framed by late-afternoon gold. Danielle. Older than he remembered. Sharper, steadier, sunlit in a way that made the whole room tilt.

She turned, the recognition instant.

"You!" she said with a grin. "The American boy who thought the city of Batroun had the best lemonade on Earth."

Adam laughed. "Still does, I hope."

Danielle worked with the regional council, coordinating supply routes, keeping flotillas fed, and negotiating among people who didn't always agree but needed one another to survive. Over the following weeks, she became Adam and Sam's guide. She led them along rebuilt cliff paths where old monasteries overlooked new floating towns, and through markets where children carved cedar charms while musicians played thin, haunting melodies on the oud. She even showed them the floating nightclub, planks lit by solar lanterns.

One evening, she nudged Adam. "Still American?"

"Still Lebanese?" he countered.

"Now more than ever."

They talked until dawn under silhouetted pines—about rebuilding, the scars of war, and the strange hope rising from drowned coastlines. She teased him for his accent; he teased her for her optimism. She said optimism was "stubbornness with lipstick." He believed her.

But Lebanon was never all romance.

One night, gunfire snapped through the air near the floating club. Danielle grabbed his hand.

"Run!"

They sprinted across bobbing platforms as stray rounds crackled above them. She laughed breathlessly as they slid behind some barrels.

"You learn to dodge bullets like mosquitoes here," she said.

Adam's heart thundered—and not just from fear.

She looked at him, eyes bright with adrenaline and mischief. For a moment, the world shrank to her laughter, her nearness, her reality. And he realized something unsettling and beautiful: She made him forget the world he'd left behind. Not erase its memory, but set it down long enough to feel present.

***

Departure came too soon.

They met near a small church overlooking the valley. Morning fog curled around the rooftops below. Danielle held Adam's hand with a softness she rarely showed.

"Maybe I'll visit," she said. "Maybe I'll make you lemonade again."

Adam smiled. "I'll hold you to that."

Their kiss was gentle—not a decision or a conclusion, but a possibility, a promise. Below them, the valley spread like a woven memory—terraces, rooftops, a thread of water sliding between stones. The newly turned mound in the cemetery glowed faintly under the early sun.

"You'll come back," she said. It was not a question.

Adam looked at her, at the hills, at the sky. "I think part of me never left."

She rolled her eyes, smiling. "That's a very Lebanese thing to say for an American boy."

They stood a moment longer on the ridge, caught between worlds, between what they were leaving and what they were returning to.

Then the moment passed.

The journey waited.

The world tugged westward.

The Return

The village had become a pocket of stability in a world that refused to sit still. The routines—refilling cisterns, checking radios, tending small plots of stubborn earth—had given their days a shape that didn't depend on tides or convoys. The mountain air carried the scent of damp soil, diesel, morning smoke, and the faint metallic tang of old tools pushed past their prime. But the water was where their missing pieces waited.

They packed light: clothes, a few tools, the bare minimum of food for the journey.

The whole town came to say goodbye. People lined the dusty road that cut through the village, shoulders brushing, eyes bright despite the early hour. Children clung to their parents' legs, not fully understanding why they were sad, only that the air felt different today—thicker, as if something were being pulled loose.

Danielle, standing near the front with her family, let a quick tear escape before she could stop it. She wiped it away with the back of her hand, as if hoping no one had seen, but Adam had. Their eyes met for a moment, and in that brief connection, a hundred unspoken things passed between them: gratitude, unanswered questions, a promise neither dared shape into words.

Sam's mother stood a little apart, her back straight, her hands folded calmly in front of her. Her eyes glistened, but no tears fell. She had decided years ago, after too many airport goodbyes and too many nights sitting alone at the window, that her son must not leave thinking he needed to worry about her. She would not send him into the world carrying guilt on top of everything else. She had learned to save her tears for after the departure, when the car or plane or ship was already gone. Grief was allowed then. It didn't get in the way.

Rami, now a trusted land captain in Sam's mind, pulled up with his infamous, reliable truck, as requested. It looked exactly as it had the last time Sam climbed into it: patched panels, wired grill, a bumper held together by stubbornness and faith. The engine idled with a sound that suggested it had opinions about being asked to make yet another trip.

"The roads, the gangs ... the crossings," Rami said as he climbed out. "Should be easier this time."

"If the world is still dangerous, we should meet it honestly," Sam replied. "But we'll be smarter. We know the routes now. The currents. The factions. Where not to linger." He turned to Adam. "Ready?"

Adam didn't hesitate. His voice was calm, but his fingers tightened on the strap of his bag. "You think I'd let you go alone?"

Sam smiled, tired and genuine—a smile full of pride, and something like an apology. "Then we'll go," he said. "We made it east. Now we return."

He lifted his voice so the nearest villagers could hear. "We'll carry this place with us," he said. "And we'll bring something back from the water—if nothing else, the truth of what we see."

A murmur of affirmation passed through the crowd. Some nodded. Some lifted their hands in blessing. Some simply watched, eyes shining.

Rami cleared his throat softly, a reminder that the road, like the sea, did not like to be kept waiting.

Goodbyes blurred into a series of quick embraces.. Adam hugged Danielle, feeling the slight tremor in her shoulders. She drew back with a crooked smile that didn't match the dampness in her eyes.

"Don't drown," she quipped.

"Don't get bored," he answered.

Adam hugged his grandmother last. She held him tighter than her age suggested she could, then pushed him away with a firm pat, as if he were still a little boy on his first day of school.

"Go," she said. "Come back when you can. Not sooner, not later. When you can."

Sam kissed her forehead, holding the moment in his chest like a breath, and he refused to let it slip. When he stepped back, his brothers moved in—not dramatically, not with tears, just with the quiet, familiar solidarity of men who understood more than they said. They pulled him into a brief, contained embrace: firm grips on shoulders, a pat on the back held a second longer than usual. Their faces stayed steady, practiced—the kind of composure you wear when the alternative is letting something deeper show.

Mark cleared his throat. "Well," he said, squeezing Sam's arm, "go easy on the pirates. They have feelings, too."

Jean smirked. "And I packed you some nausea pills. Take them an hour before a hurricane hits."

Sam shook his head, muted smile flickering. The jokes were thin, almost intentionally so—minor detours meant to keep the heaviness from settling too squarely on any of them.

For a moment, they lingered like that—hands on shoulders, the air tight with everything left unsaid. The humor held the line, giving them just enough space to stay steady, to keep the sadness tucked neatly behind the familiar rhythm of brotherly banter. Sam let the quiet strength of it anchor him, knowing precisely what sat beneath every restrained smile.

Then they climbed into the truck. As it pulled away, the village grew smaller in the side mirrors: stone houses, clustered lights, the outline of people standing at the edge of the road and waving until their arms grew tired. Faces faded into shapes, then colors, then nothing at all.

Adam kept his eyes on the fading silhouettes until the last roof dipped below the ridge. He turned forward only when there was nothing left to hold onto but memory.

The road bent westward. Behind them, the mountains did not disappear. They settled into the back of Sam's mind, becoming what they had been for him all along—wounds and blessing alike. Some places stayed with you, even when you left them behind. Some goodbyes never finished; they just grew quieter with distance. And some decisions—about where you belonged, and with whom—would have to wait until the sea had finished telling its side of the story.

Leaving the mountains felt, in some ways, harder than leaving the sea.

Rami drove them back toward the coast. In the sharp daylight, the road looked different from how Sam remembered it in the darkness of their first crossing. They could see the jagged edges where rockslides had clawed pieces of the hillside away. Fresh rockfalls still littered the shoulders. Old guardrails had been ripped away in places and replaced with nothing but painted warnings and a few stacked tires that wouldn't stop a truck so much as mark the spot where it had once gone over.

"Remember," Rami said as they descended, his eyes never leaving the road, "land has its own pirates. Don't trust uniforms alone. Trust eyes, hands, and how people stand. Fear and greed look the same everywhere."

Sam nodded. "We've met their cousins on the sea."

Near the halfway point, they spotted a roadblock—a makeshift barrier of cars dragged sideways across the asphalt, their doors removed to make room for armed men. They leaned against the metal with the languid confidence of people who knew the road belonged to them more than to any government.

"Slow," Rami murmured, "but not too slow."

Too slow looked nervous. Too fast looked hostile.

He rolled down his window as they approached.

The men wore mismatched gear—civilian jackets, pieces of old military vests, scarves wrapped over their mouths. Their rifles were clean, but their boots were scuffed from use. This wasn't theater. This was their office.

"Where are you headed?" one asked. His Arabic was clipped, efficient. His eyes flicked between Sam, Adam, and Rami, measuring more than their answers.

"Down to the port," Rami said. "Family has passage. We're not carrying anything worth stealing, unless you like dirty socks."

One of the men smirked, but did not lower his weapon. "Everyone is carrying something of worth these days," he said. "Supplies. Information. Hope."

He let the last word hang in the air like a challenge.

Sam understood the dynamic instinctively: show neither fear nor arrogance. Fear invited cruelty. Arrogance invited correction. Survival lived somewhere in between.

"We're not important," Sam said. He kept his voice level, his gaze steady but not confrontational. "Just a father and son trying to find the rest of our family."

The man studied him for a heartbeat longer. There was calculation in his eyes—and fatigue. Finally, he nodded to the others.

"Let them pass," he said. "We have enough trouble for today."

The barrier shifted just enough for the truck to squeeze through. As they rolled forward, tires crunching over cracked asphalt and gravel, Adam exhaled the breath he'd been holding.

"That could've gone differently."

"It still might, at the next one," Rami replied. "Remember this: the flood didn't wash away human nature. It just gave it new uniforms."

Closer to the coast, the sound changed again. The low hum of wind over rock gave way to the distant, familiar roar of water. Not the gentle lapping of a lake, but the deep, continuous breath of a swollen sea that had swallowed continents and refused to give them back. The air grew heavier, tinged with salt and the smell of fuel.

The port itself felt more crowded, more tense than when they'd first arrived weeks ago. There were more guards now, more fences, more signs written in three languages warning about unauthorized crossings, smuggling, and piracy. The attempt at order only highlighted how fragile it was.

"Business is good," Adam said dryly, watching lines of people snake toward different piers, some carrying bags, others carrying nothing but each other.

"Depends on the business," Sam replied.

They found their ship by its shape and sound before they saw its name—a medium-sized vessel that had clearly been something else before the flood. Its original identity was obscured beneath layers of hastily welded plates, extra fuel tanks, and a cluster of small, battered lifeboats lashed along its sides like barnacles. Men and women moved along its gangway with the efficiency of people who had learned that hesitation could get you killed. Crates were loaded, manifest lists were shouted, and decisions about who would board and who would wait were made with quick, brutal finality.

On the far side of the port, two groups of armed men shouted at each other near a stack of shipping containers. The argument escalated from words to gestures to curses, then to rifles raised in a matter of seconds.

"Keep your head down," Sam said, putting a hand on Adam's shoulder. "And keep moving."

They hurried up the gangway as crew members shouted for people to choose: board now or stay behind. The deck thrummed beneath their feet, the vibrations of engines warming up traveling through steel into bone.

Once on deck, Sam leaned against the rail for a heartbeat, catching his breath. Below, port security moved toward the confrontation with weary urgency.

"Business as usual," Adam said quietly. There was no humor in it.

The ship's horn bellowed a long, low sound that vibrated in their ribs. Lines were thrown off. Engines rumbled more insistently. The port began to recede, shrinking into a jagged line of cranes, rooftops, and desperate negotiations.

Ahead of them, the water waited like a old friend.

Adam watched the coastline pull away, his expression a complicated mix of dread and relief. "I thought I was done with this," he said.

"So did I," Sam answered. "But the things that matter to us are not evenly distributed between land and sea. We have to follow them, wherever they drift."

He looked out at the horizon. The surface was deceptively calm, but Sam now knew how little that meant. He carried the charts in his mind—the currents, the submerged ruins, the places where a ship could vanish without anyone ever seeing it go.

The world was still broken. Gangs still patrolled the cliffs. Militias still squabbled over scraps of land and power. The sea still carried secrets and debris in equal measure. But they were no longer drifting. They had chosen a direction. Toward someone. Toward the next chapter of the story.

***

Nights at sea felt different this time.

The first crossing had been a desperate search—a blind push into uncertainty with water on all sides and grief pressing from behind. This voyage carried another weight: the knowledge of what waited on either shore. The fear was still there, but it had changed shape, now sharing space with expectation.

They slept in shifts, not because the crew demanded it, but because neither of them could fully surrender to rest. Each creak of the hull, each change in the engine's tone, each murmur from other passengers threaded into their dreams and tugged them halfway back to waking.

The next morning, before the sun made its presence known, when the sea had settled into a slow, heavy roll and most of the ship's passengers were either asleep or pretending to be, Sam and Adam stood at the rail, watching the reflection of lights from fishing boats quiver on the dark surface. The air was cool and salty. The world felt suspended.

"It's strange," Adam said. "Up there, the universe looks the same. Same constellations. Same light. If you showed me that sky without context, I could almost believe nothing had changed."

"Maybe that's a mercy," Sam said. "Or maybe it's a reminder."

"Of what?"

"That scale is relative," Sam answered. "Our catastrophe doesn't even smudge their map."

Adam considered that. "Comforting."

"In a way," Sam said. "If the universe had flinched when we were flooded, I'd be more worried. It would mean we were more important than we really are."

A soft gust of wind pushed against them, making the railing hum for a moment. Somewhere below, metal groaned as the ship adjusted to a deeper swell.

They fell into a quiet that wasn't empty, but full of unspoken thoughts.

After a while, Sam said, "I've been thinking about your space fabric again."

Adam smiled, the expression faint but genuine. "You have?"

"I keep coming back to this," Sam said. "You said once that matter twists space, and when stars burn, they reach equilibrium. But what if that's what we're supposed to do, too? Not as physics, but as people."

"Twist the universe?" Adam joked.

"Reach equilibrium," Sam clarified. "Between what we take and what we give. Between what we destroy and what we repair. Between fear and hope."

He leaned on the rail, fingers curled around the cold metal.

"Before the flood, we twisted the world too much," he went on. "We took and took. We stretched systems until they snapped. Maybe the flood wasn't just ice and orbits. Maybe it was fabric snapping back," Sam said softly. "Untwisting."

"Interesting," Adam said. "And now we're in the slack afterwards, trying to decide how we're going to twist it next time. If we learned anything."

"This sounds like we're part of the equation," Sam said.

"Aren't we?" Adam asked. "We keep pretending we're outside the system, looking in. Observers. But we're in the batter, Dad. We're ingredients."

Sam watched his son, pride and awe mingling quietly inside him. There were moments—like this one—when he saw the boy Adam had been and the man he was becoming at the same time, layered over each other like two images slightly out of sync.

Sam's gaze drifted upward again to the stars. The idea had comforted him since Adam first talked about the "Universe Cake"—a state where separation blurred, where space and time and matter and energy were just flavors in the same mix. In that state, all the borders and flags and debts and grudges they fought over down here wouldn't make sense anymore.

"Maybe that's the lesson," Adam said.

Sam turned back to him. "Which one?"

"That if we keep twisting only for ourselves," Adam said, "we get the same ending. Floods. Wars. Gangs at checkpoints. Pirates on cliffs. People dancing in night clubs while bullets fly. It becomes … business as usual."

"And the alternative?" Sam asked.

Adam shrugged lightly. "We twist differently. We plan cities that expect water, not pretend it isn't coming. We build floating towns that aren't just lifeboats, but places to live. We treat Mars as a partner, not an escape pod. We preserve stories and seeds and songs with the same efficiency as fuel and steel." He looked at Sam. "We treat survival as the minimum, not the goal."

Sam let the words settle between them. The ship creaked again, a slow, tired stretch, as if the hull itself were listening.

"Do you think people will do that?" he asked.

"Some will," Adam said. "Some already are. Haven-3. Those mountain depots. The seed vaults. The villages that share their high ground instead of selling it. The crews that risk run-ins with pirates to ferry strangers."

"And the others?" Sam pushed gently.

Adam's mouth twisted in a grim half-smile. "Some will keep playing the old games in a new arena. Gangsters on the cliffs. Strongmen on the hills. People who sell life jackets at a profit during a storm. I don't think that ever goes away completely."

"Then what's the point?" Sam asked. There was no despair in the question, just an honest curiosity.

Adam took a breath, tasting salt and diesel and something like determination. "The point is that now we know the difference," he said. "Before, it was easy to pretend it didn't matter. To tell ourselves the planet could absorb anything, that the poor places were far away, that the storms were someone else's problem. The flood took that away. It made the consequences impossible to ignore." He gestured toward the dark water. "We're sailing through our own report card."

Sam laughed once, softly. "Harsh teacher."

"Fair teacher," Adam said. "We built a world that could drown this way. Now we have to build one that can float and still recognize itself."

They stood in silence a while longer, listeners on the deck of their own thoughts. The ship rolled gently. Someone coughed on the far side of the deck. A door shut. The world continued its small, ordinary sounds beneath the vastness of their conversation.

Finally, Sam spoke.

"When I first saw the anomaly," he said, "I thought my job was to warn people. Then I thought it was to help them prepare. Then I thought it was to help them survive."

He exhaled slowly. The breath scraped a little on the way out.

"Now I think my job might just be to remember," he said. "To tell the truth about what happened. To whoever is willing to listen. On Earth. On Mars. In floating cities. In mountain villages. In places we haven't built yet."

Adam nodded. "You'll be good at that," he said. "You already are."

Sam shook his head. "I didn't do enough."

"Maybe nobody could have," Adam replied. "You can't untwist the whole universe by yourself. But you can show people where the fabric tore." He glanced at his father. "And you can tell them how it feels to stand at the edge and not fall in."

The horizon ahead brightened with the first hint of dawn—a thin, gray line peeling night away from day. Somewhere beyond it, another port would be waiting.

"Do you ever think," Adam said slowly, "that the universe is giving us another chance?"

Sam considered that. "I think the universe is indifferent," he said. "But I think life isn't. We're the part that cares. That's our job." He put a hand on Adam's shoulder. "Maybe that's the lesson."

Adam smiled faintly. "That we're not the center of the universe, but we are the center of our own choices."

"And that sometimes," Sam added, "the bravest thing you can do isn't to run from the storm, but to sail back into it, knowing what it can do, because someone you love is on the other side."

The sun pushed higher, bleeding color into the clouds. The water shifted from black to deep blue, then to something lighter, more forgiving. In that slow brightening, Sam felt the presence of everyone they carried with them: Eisha and Sarah, somewhere ahead; his mother, somewhere behind; Barlow and the crews and the strangers who had shared their decks and risks; the billions whose stories would never be written down, but lived on in the angle of a rebuilt roof, the curve of a new hull, the way a child learned to read tide charts before textbooks.

The world was not what it had been. It never would be again. But beneath the altered sky and above the swollen sea, two figures stood at the rail of a ship moving through the aftermath, determined to twist the fabric of their small corner of the universe in a direction that made survival mean more than not dying.

"Until next time," Sam murmured, almost to himself, thinking of all the people the phrase now applied to.

They stayed there a little longer, watching the day unwrap itself. Eventually, the deck grew busier—footsteps, voices, the clatter of breakfast being prepared somewhere below.

"Go eat," Sam said. "I'll join you in a bit."

"You sure?" Adam asked.

Sam nodded. "There's something I need to do while the sky is still honest."

Adam hesitated, then squeezed his father's arm and headed toward the stairs.

When Sam was alone again, he let the quiet settle around him. The sea whispered against the hull. The sky, now fully awake, stretched wide and indifferent.

He turned away from the rail and walked back toward their small cabin.

Inside, the room felt even narrower than before, walls close, air faintly warm from their sleep. Sam sat at the small desk where the light from the slim porthole cut a pale strip across the metal surface. He powered on the console and waited for the dim screen to glow to life. The ship's comms still showed no active link—not yet—but he knew from experience that messages could be written and queued, ready to leap outward the moment the ship brushed against a working network.

He opened a blank message window and stared at the cursor for a long moment.

Eisha, he typed. The name alone loosened something in his chest.

He rested his fingers lightly on the keys, feeling the weight of everything he needed to say. Some things were practical. Some were logistical. Some were the kind of truths you only allow yourself to write when there is no one watching your face.

He began.

I'm writing this while the sea is calm and the sky is pretending that nothing has changed. If you could see it from here, you'd say it looks like it did before the flood. But you and I know better now. We've seen what sits underneath.

He told her about his father first. He wrote about the last time he'd seen the old man awake—the way his hands had softened, the way his words had grown shorter, but somehow weightier. How he had pretended to be stronger than he felt, so his son wouldn't worry, the same way Sam's mother saved her tears so he wouldn't carry them with him.

He's gone now, Sam wrote. *He slipped away the way mountains fade in the rearview—slow, then all at once. I was there. It was quiet. He wasn't afraid. I think ... I think he knew I did everything I could to reach him before it was too late.*

For a moment, Sam's vision blurred. He blinked until the words steadied again.

I wasn't sure if I should tell you, he continued, *not by message, because I didn't want you and Sarah to grieve in the same breath as the flood. I wanted you to have room to breathe between storms. But you should know now. You would have liked the way he faced the end. It was stubborn and gentle at the same time.*

He paused, letting the memory settle.

Then he wrote about the village, the routines, the stubborn earth that insisted on providing food even after the world had drowned. He told her about Danielle, about his mother's dry eyes at the roadside, about the way the whole town had come to see them off as if they were not just two travelers, but messengers carrying a piece of the mountain world with them.

He explained the road, the checkpoint, the men who understood that hope itself was a kind of contraband.

He described the port—crowded, tense, small wars breaking out in the shadow of larger ones—and the ship they had boarded. He softened some details for her sake, sharpened others for honesty's sake. He did not mention everybody on the ground. He did not need to. Eisha knew how to read between his lines.

Then he came to the part he knew would hurt her, but would also prepare her.

We are heading back east, he wrote. *I wish I could tell you we are coming directly home, that the sea between us is short and simple. But the world will not allow that yet.*

He laid it out plainly, the way he always had, letting the data speak for itself.

Europe has become too dangerous, he wrote. *The northern corridors are fractured—raids, shortages, old powers trying to act like new ones. What used to be routes is now a trap. Africa is … still a mystery. Some signals, some stories, too few guarantees. Enough rumor to tempt a reckless man, not enough truth to justify taking you and Sarah into it blind.*

His fingers tightened on the edge of the desk.

So, we keep going east, he went on. *Not because we're running away, but because sometimes the safest way home is the long way around. We'll follow calmer waters, quieter ports, places that are rebuilding instead of tearing themselves apart. It will take longer. I hate that. But I love you even more than I hate waiting. So, I will choose the path that gives us the best chance of all being in the same room again.*

He hesitated, then added:

Tell Sarah that the sky still looks like the one she remembers. Tell her that the stars are still in the same places, even if we are not. Tell her that when I look up, I see the same patterns we traced for her when she was little on the deck of the old lake house—and that I follow them the same way I follow the thought of you both.

He let his hands rest.

Outside, the sea kept its slow, patient rhythm. Somewhere down the corridor, a child laughed. Elsewhere, someone cursed at a stuck latch. Life, reduced and rearranged, went on.

Sam scrolled back through what he had written. There was more he could add—about the twisting of the fabric, about report cards written in coastlines—but this message, he knew, was not the place for lectures. This was for love and truth.

He let his hands rest on the keys, and for a moment, simply sat there. He thought of his mother, probably somewhere with a cup of tea, allowing herself at last to cry where no one could see. He thought of Danielle's single, hurried tear. He thought of his father's last steady breath. He thought of Eisha and Sarah, somewhere ahead, lighting their own small candles against the dark.

Outside, the ship moved steadily east, its wake carving a temporary line between what they had left behind and what they were sailing toward. For now, that line—and the people waiting at both ends—was enough.

At the end, he wrote:

When the radios crackle with your names, I'll be there to hear it. Until then, imagine me standing at the rail, the way we always did when we left Lebanon. One last look. Then another. Then another. Home behind us, home ahead of us, you somewhere in between, keeping the line from breaking.

Until next time,

Sam.

THE HUMAN BEHIND THE STORY

Author's Note

The heart of this novel—the fears, hopes, memories, and emotional truths—comes entirely from my own life.

This story began long before I ever typed a word. It started in Lebanon, during years of war, when nights were interrupted by the sudden thunder of bombs. My family kept a briefcase by the door filled with everything we couldn't afford to lose—documents, land deeds, gold, cash. When the shelling started, whoever reached it first grabbed the bag and shouted "I've got it!", and we ran for shelter.

We lived with the knowledge that everything we loved could vanish in a moment. That sense of sudden disaster and forced escape lives inside this book.

War also taught me about separation. Families, neighbors, and entire communities could be scattered across the world overnight. This was the 1980s—no social media, no easy way to stay in touch. If someone you loved fled to Australia and you ended up in America, how would you ever find them again? That fear of losing the people who give meaning to your world runs deep through the pages of *Ocean Earth*.

Another deep root of this story is my father.

He is still alive as I write this, but he has been bedridden with dementia for some time. The past few years have been a cycle of phone calls, worry, and sudden trips back to Lebanon—each time wondering whether it would be the last visit. After his fall and stroke, I received photos that made it look like he wouldn't survive. I flew home. He recognized me. That recognition—fragile but unmistakable—felt like a miracle. Later, I brought my kids, and he recognized them too. Each visit felt like God opening one more window just long enough for one more blessing.

Leaving was always the most challenging part. I remember standing at the bottom of the stairs during one trip, looking up at him as he leaned weakly on the railing. We looked at each other with the same unspoken question: *Is this the last time we will see each other alive?* That moment stayed with me long after I boarded the plane back to the United States.

Even in his condition, he never failed to recognize my mother's voice. And in one precise moment, he asked her: "Do you think I'll ever see my kids again?" My sister in Canada. Me in the U.S. Children scattered by life.

That single question—the fear of never seeing your loved ones again—became the emotional heartbeat of Ocean Earth. Behind every reunion, every search, every desperate hope in this novel is a real feeling from my own life: the longing to see family one more time.

Ocean Earth is a translation of those experiences into another language.

The storm is the war.

The survival kit is the briefcase by the door.

The hurried convoys are the sudden departures that scattered families across continents.

And the long conversations shared during evenings at home come from my favorite part of childhood: nights spent with a large family gathered together, talking and laughing.

I didn't invent those dynamics. I lived them. I only changed their scale.

But the book is not only about loss. It is also about wonder.

As a child, I spent nights lying on the roof of our mountain home, tracing the Milky Way with my eyes, counting shooting stars, and dreaming about distant galaxies. I read astronomy magazines, and later in life, I bought a telescope for my kids (though I was the one who used it). My fascination with space, consciousness, and the mysteries of the universe shaped many of the scientific reflections woven into this story.

And then there are the works of art that raised me: *Sinbad the Sailor*, *Mad Max*, *Indiana Jones*, *Crocodile Dundee*, *Jewel of the Nile*, *Tintin*—adventure stories from the 1970s and 1980s—fun, hopeful, full of heart. I've never liked darkness for its own sake. Even in the face of catastrophe, I believe life can be beautiful, funny, and resilient. That's why *Ocean Earth* offers danger without cynicism, challenge without despair. The world floods, yes—but humanity improvises, adapts, and survives.

This novel also carries the emotional tension of my own life: I love the United States, and I love Lebanon. Leaving one to live in the other was never simple. Even now, both places feel like home—and both places feel like loss. That push and pull—the feeling of being rooted in two worlds—is part of this story's DNA.

When I first shared the idea of *Ocean Earth* with my wife, she loved it instantly. Her encouragement lit the spark. And once I started writing—with AI as a tool to help me structure the work—I became fully immersed. But the story, the themes, the emotional core… Those are all me. AI didn't imagine the flood, the families, the convoys, the scientific wonder, the tender reunions. It only helped me turn my experiences into a structured manuscript.

The drowned world you read about is fictional. But the heart behind it is real.

I hope this glimpse into my life shows you that behind the boats and storms and cosmic mysteries, there is a human story—*my* story—driving every page of *Ocean Earth*.

—Sam Terra

"HOMEMADE SCIENCE"

Concepts Behind Ocean Earth

Curiosity doesn't end when the story does. These "homemade science" reflections are not intended as proven physics, but as imaginative thought experiments—a blend of speculative science, metaphor, and human curiosity.

Accordingly, the main interrelated concepts explored in this section are:

- The Universe Cake Concept
- The Black Hole Medium
- The Twisting and Untwisting Hypothesis
- $E = mc^2$ at Space–Matter Equilibrium
- Observation, Waves, and the Medium of Reality

Other speculative ideas include:

- The "Top" and "Bottom" of Our World
- Consciousness Is the Fifth Dimension, and Life Is a Force
- Instantaneity and the Center of the Universe
- The Purpose of Homemade Science

The Interrelated Concepts

Two Fundamental States of the Universe

Imagine the universe operating in two different states. In the first state—the one we experience—space, time, matter, light, and energy exist as separate ingredients, each behaving according to rules we can measure and describe. In the second state, those ingredients no longer exist in the way our conservation-based physics requires—a deliberate violation in this homemade model—or they become so thoroughly blended that the distinctions between them fade or disappear.

What remains is a single, unified medium in which our everyday categories no longer behave the same way. In other words, if the universe can begin from a state we describe as "nothing," then in this homemade model, it may also be able to return to a similar state—one where the rules of our ingredient universe no longer apply.

This breakdown of familiar rules is also hinted at in the double-slit experiment, where particles do not follow classical paths and behave as if the usual expectations of space, time, and motion are only partial descriptions of their reality. A similar hint appears in quantum entanglement, where two particles separated by vast distances seem to share a single state, responding to each other in ways that ignore the limits of distance and the timing our everyday physics depends on.

This idea forms the basis of the **Universe Cake** concept: on our side of reality, we have space, fabric, matter, energy, and light (flour, sugar, eggs…); inside a black hole, the cake has already been baked, possibly into "nothingness."

The Black Hole as a New Medium

A black hole becomes a new medium, with the event horizon marking the boundary between these two states, where the familiar fabric of spacetime is no longer available. Light has no space to travel through. Matter has no location to occupy. Time has no sequence to follow. In this homemade view, a black hole is not necessarily an object with extreme gravity; it is a new medium, with either a blended state of all the universe's ingredients—or possibly nothingness.

This leads to a speculative question: if $E = mc^2$ links mass and energy in our world, what does that relationship become once the "cake" has formed? Could E effectively approach zero inside a black hole, if neither mass nor light can exist due to the absence of their natural habitat—the space fabric itself?

Light, Medium, and the Fate of Matter

A key idea follows from this view: light may not fail to escape a black hole because gravity pulls it back, but because the medium light requires—space itself—has changed or is no longer available. Without usable space, a "path" no longer exists. Matter faces the same fate: without space to inhabit, the very meaning of location breaks down.

The Mass-Loss Paradox in Star Collapse

Traditional theory says massive stars burn fuel, lose mass, expand, become unstable, and then collapse into an incredibly dense object. But if mass is decreasing, and therefore gravitational pull weakens, how does the final collapse generate such extreme gravitational effects?

The conventional answer involves density, pressure, and the limits of quantum forces. The homemade perspective proposes something different: the collapse may depend less on "more gravity" and more on the interaction between matter and the space fabric.

Curving, Twisting, and Untwisting the Space Fabric

Matter bends the space fabric. In this speculative model, it may also twist it. As stars lose mass, their grip on space fabric weakens. Eventually, a balance or tipping point is reached—a fragile moment where the tug-of-war between matter and space is even. When the star can no longer maintain its grip, space may untwist catastrophically, snapping back like a released spring. This untwisting could create the transition that forms a black hole—a tear, a collapse, or the beginning of a new medium.

In this scenario, the black hole's extreme environment is not produced by extreme gravity, but by the structural response of space itself.

The Strength of the Space Fabric

This raises another question: what is the "strength" of the space fabric? If a moment of equilibrium exists in the matter–space interaction, perhaps $E = mc^2$ could help approximate it. We know c. If we can estimate the mass of a dying star at equilibrium, could we then calculate the "yield point" of space itself?

Observation, Waves, and the Medium of Reality

The double-slit experiment raises a deceptively simple question: what does it actually mean to "observe" a particle? When the experiment is run, and the results are recorded, electrons produce an interference pattern—a wave-like behavior. When measuring equipment is introduced to determine which slit the electron passes through, its behavior changes, and the wave-particle appears to behave like matter, following a single path.

This suggests that "observation" is not about awareness itself, but about physical interaction. The receiving screen at the end of the experiment can be counted as a form of physical (not conscious) observer. In the wave case, the screen records an interference pattern, meaning that something physical—energy or matter—is still striking it. The difference is not whether it is matter, but how it behaves.

One way to think about this is to treat waves not as something separate from matter, but as matter in motion. A useful analogy is water. The surface of water is matter. Drop a stone into it, and waves form. The peaks and valleys of those waves are not abstract—they are physical displacements of water. When two waves meet, they interfere: some regions grow stronger, others cancel out. Yet the water itself never disappears. Introduce an additional disturbance into the surface, and the behavior changes again. We are essentially interfering with the "matter-wave continuum," the medium.

From this perspective, light—and even electrons—may be understood as matter or energy propagating through a medium by vibration. The wave pattern in the double-slit experiment reflects how this vibration spreads through it, producing regions of reinforcement and cancellation rather than the absence or presence of matter.

This leads to a crucial idea: the measuring apparatus may not be changing the behavior of the particle itself, but disturbing the medium through which it travels. When additional detectors or electronic equipment are introduced, they interact with the space fabric—altering the conditions that allow wave-like behavior to form. Much like another disturbance introduced to the surface of water, inserting measuring devices modifies how matter or energy vibrates through space, and the observed behavior changes as a result.

In this homemade view, observation is not a mystical act of consciousness collapsing reality, but a physical interaction that modifies the environment. The particle responds to what the medium allows. When the medium is undisturbed, wave behavior emerges. When the medium is altered by measurement, the behavior shifts toward what we interpret as particle-like.

This perspective also offers an intuitive way to think about entanglement. When particles appear to share a single state across distance, it may not be that information is traveling instantaneously, but that they remain linked through a shared structure of the underlying medium, even as they appear separated—an effect resembling reflections by a distorted surface.

None of these claims replaces established physics. This is simply an attempt to reframe familiar experiments by shifting attention away from particles alone and toward the medium that makes their behavior possible. In homemade science, asking what is being disturbed can be as important as asking what is being observed.

Other Speculative Ideas

The "Top," "Bottom," "Front," and "Back" of Our World

In space, direction has no meaning. Without a point of reference, there is no up, down, front, or back. But our solar system moves through the galaxy at high speed. Motion becomes a point of reference: the direction we travel toward is the front, the opposite the rear, and the ecliptic plane defines a rough "up" and "down." Because the North Pole aligns roughly with our direction of travel, it can be called the "top" of our world in this homemade framework. This is not absolute—just a perspective born from motion.

Consciousness is the Fifth Dimension, and Life is a Force

We experience three spatial dimensions and one temporal dimension. These four shape every physical interaction we observe. But there is a fifth dimension we also feel directly: consciousness. It does not behave like length, width, height, or time, yet removing it makes our entire human universe meaningless. A world without consciousness is not a world anyone could experience.

In this homemade view, a "dimension" is something that must exist for a system to make sense to the beings inside it. By that test, consciousness qualifies. Mathematical or theoretical dimensions beyond our perception are interesting, but less intuitive; consciousness is immediate and undeniable. It shapes the reality we interpret, and without it, the known universe collapses into irrelevance.

This leads to a related idea: life itself behaves like a force. We study gravity, electromagnetism, and nuclear forces with equations and laws, yet life exerts influence in its own unmistakable way. A sprout breaking through concrete to reach the sun is not a metaphor; it is an expression of something persistent, directional, and powerful. Life pushes. Life climbs. Life selects, adapts, and persists.

In this homemade model, life may be viewed as a physical force that deserves study with the same rigor as the others—perhaps even with its own formulas. If consciousness is the fifth dimension that makes experience possible, then life may be the force that makes consciousness possible.

Instantaneity and the Center of the Universe

Nothing travels faster than light (except the universe's expansion). Everything we see far away is actually how it appeared long ago. The universe we observe is a record of events that no longer exist. Each observer sits at the center of their own sphere of "now," surrounded by a fading bubble of earlier moments. In practice, everyone is the center of their own observable universe.

Homemade Science

Homemade science is not about being right; it is about asking anyway. These ideas are offered in that spirit—not as truth, but as invitations. Question them, reshape them, bake them again. The universe, after all, is still cooking.